Contents

1. Dina 1
2. The Execution Day 5
3. The Slave's Execution 9
4. Dina, the God's Gift 13
5. The Tomb 18
6. 1940, Berlin 22
7. 1940, Egypt 27
8. The Rivals 30
9. The Excavation Site 35
10. The Tomb 40
11. The Next Steps 44
12. The New Crew 48
13. Inside 54
14. Anubis 61
15. Dina 65
16. The Search for the Heart Scarab Starts 69
17. The Tombs of Nobles 74
18. The Mummies 82

19. Dina 86
20. Hotel Alhambra 90
21. Jack and Sawyer 97
22. The New Plan 100
23. The Zeppelin 103
24. Inside the Blimp 109
25. The Flight 115
26. At Himmler's Office 121
27. Inside the Blimp 127
28. Dina's New Allies 131
29. In Berlin 136
30. Landing in Berlin 139
31. At the Airport 143
32. Helmut's Mistake 150
33. Enemies or Friends? 153
34. Jack, Sawyer, and the Others 157
35. The Warehouse 161
36. One Day Gone, Two Left 165
37. More Mummies 169
38. Dina's Fear 173
39. Where to Go Next? 176
40. Driving Around Berlin 180
41. Himmler 186

The Lost Tomb

Arla Jones

This book is a work of fiction. Names, characters, businesses, organizations, places, events, and incidents either are the product of the author's imagination or are used fictitiously. Any resemblance to actual persons, living or dead, events, or locales is entirely coincidental. Even though the book has some historical figures, the events and interactions with the characters are purely fictional.

1st Edition 2024

Editor: Kate Seger

The header image by Lauren N Hanson

The map by RDH Cover Designs

The cover by TMT Cover Designs

This has been previously published as a serial fiction story on Kindle Vella.

I would like to express my special thanks to my editor Kate Seger, my talented header illustrator Lauren, my cover designer TMT Cover Designs, and my map creator RDH Cover Designs.

42. Himmler Meets Jack and Carl 192
43. Dina's Decision 200
44. Dina and Sawyer 204
45. A Drive Through Berlin 208
46. The Attack 211
47. What Happened? 217
48. The Mummy Ride 223
49. Anubis Returns 231
50. The New Plan 236
51. The Nazis 239
52. The Drive 248
53. The Prisoners 251
54. Osiris 258
55. The Elevator 262
56. The Germans 268
About the author 274
Also By The Author 275

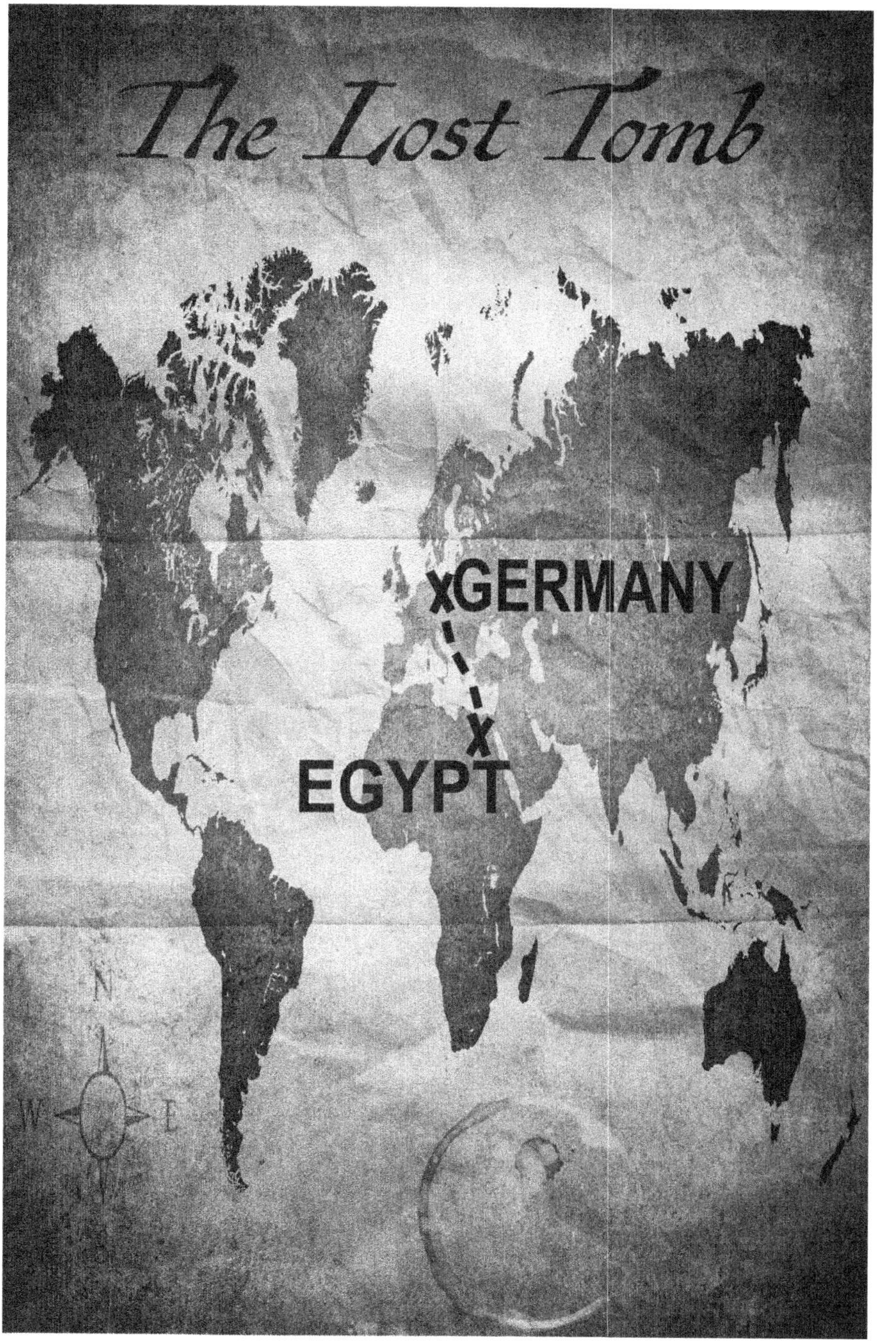
The Lost Tomb
xGERMANY
EGYPT
N
W
E

1

Dina

1300 BC in Ancient Egypt

The palace was busy as the pharaoh returned from his trip to the Nile, where he paid homage to Hapi, the god of fishes and water, and he had prayed for Min for plentiful crops for the coming season. Next, it was time to sacrifice a virgin to the river Nile to appease the gods.

His high priest, Thutmose, paced impatiently in the great hallway glancing worriedly toward a closed door behind him. He was a tall and skinny man with a bald head. He bore the symbols of priesthood in his white robe and wore a jewel-decorated broad-collar necklace and golden bracelets decorated with images of the Egyptian gods.

His daughter, Dina, was inside. "Dina, get ready. Pharaoh Akhenaten is coming. His entourage is at the gate now!" he called to his daughter. No answer. He knocked on the door and then tried to open it. It was locked. Frowning, he gestured for the three pharaoh's guards in the hallway to help him open the door. They put aside their spears and pushed the door with their shoulders over and over again until it broke open. They stumbled inside, quickly turning their faces to the ground. The sight was not what they expected to see or were allowed to view.

Thutmose ambled inside and surveyed the room, and to his horror, Dina was in the bed, half-naked in the arms of a slave! His beautiful daughter! The promised virgin gift to the gods!

"No, Dina! You shouldn't have done this. You're pledged to be a virgin! You'll be sacrificed to the river Nile for a bountiful year. The pharaoh is coming to get you and is at the gates!" Thutmose rushed to the bedside, grabbed Dina by the arm, and slapped her on the cheek, leaving a red mark. Dina turned her dark eyes to her father rebelliously. Her bead-decorated and braided black hair reached past her shoulders to her hips. Her eyes were shadowed with black kohl, and her lips were colored with red ochre. Her blue dress, decorated with golden threads made especially for the sacrifice ceremony, lay on the floor by the bedside.

The slave, Aper, rose and bowed his head. Thutmose was a powerful man in the palace, and he was only a slave. He was not supposed to look at

Dina or want her, but he had. He had destroyed her life and his own. He knew it, and he waited for punishment.

"No, father. I love Aper!" Dina exclaimed, pulling her arm away and grabbing the sheets to cover her upper body. She leaned forward to take Aper's hand, but he stepped back, shaking his head and looking mortified.

Dina's face was distorted with emotions. *Aper pulled away from me! My father is raging, and the pharaoh is at the gate! What do I do?* She sat up, keeping the sheet in front of her, and then asked her father, "What can I do?"

"Nothing." Her father looked devastated. He gestured to the guards, who kept their eyes on the floor, and commanded, "Take the slave and behead him."

Two of the guards approached Aper and grabbed him by the arms. He didn't resist because he knew he had done wrong.

Dina cried, "No! I love him! Don't do this!"

"I have no choice. You did this to yourself." Her father faced her and then told the last guard standing by the doorway, "My daughter remains here. Guard her."

Thutmose walked outside and met the pharaoh's entourage outside the palace. He kneeled in front of the pharaoh. "My god, I have sad news for you."

"What is it?" Akhenaten asked coldly. His high priest had acted out of order. He was tasked to get his daughter for the ceremony, but he was here without her.

"My pharaoh, my daughter Dina is no longer suitable for the sacrifice," Thutmose said, keeping his eyes on the floor. He was not allowed to look into the pharaoh's eyes. He was a god on earth.

"She'll be sentenced to death. She'll be buried alive in the new tomb we built. You need to prepare her for that destiny. You will be killed if you don't do that," Akhenaten replied angrily. "The gods will be angry. We need to find another sacrifice."

Thutmose paled. He felt a shiver run through his body, but he didn't move. *How can I kill my daughter? I was told to prepare her to be buried alive! This is the most horrible destiny I can imagine. How can I tell her?*

"You are dismissed," Akhenaten stated and gestured to his slaves and guards to turn his entourage toward the palace entrance. He was annoyed. The sacrifice ceremony would have to be rescheduled because of that inconsiderate, harum-scarum daughter of the high priest.

Akhenaten glanced back at his Thutmose and wondered if he should do something to him, too, because the betrayal of the gods could bring their wrath down upon the whole land.

2

The Execution Day

The day Dina and the slave are to be killed

Thutmose took his morning ritual bath to clean himself, then with the help of slaves, he got dressed in his most impressive high priest's outfit: A white robe with golden adornments of the ancient symbols. He sighed as he took his high priest symbols: the scepter decorated with golden wings and the black book of Anubis, the god of the dead, with him. He didn't bring the golden book of Ra with him. There was no need. This was the day for the curses and to pray for the god of the dead to help his daughter, Dina.

It was the day to slaughter the obnoxious slave who had destroyed his daughter.

The book was usually never carried out of the priests' temple complex.

The palace had informed him that the pharaoh would also come to see the execution of the slave and the entombment of Dina, who had betrayed the pharaoh, and the crowd had gathered along the river Nile to see the rare execution. It was not every day that a high priest's daughter would be killed by her father.

Dina's lover, the slave Aper, had been escorted to the riverside by the pharaoh's soldiers. The guards stood next to him in full body armor with spears in their hands in case the prisoner tried to escape. Aper was on his knees with his head bowed. His strong upper body shone with sweat. Red welts and dried blood streaked his back from a recent whipping. Aper's face was solemn; he knew his fate. He had known it since he met Dina.

Dina was imprisoned in the dungeons of the pharaoh's palace, situated at the bottom of the palace complex. It had no wall paintings or statues like the upper floors, only a plain hallway leading to the prisoners' area, with guards watching the exits.

A group of lower-level priests followed Thutmose to the dungeon hallway, and two guards joined him to get Dina. The pharaoh had ordered Dina to watch her lover be executed before she faced her death. Thutmose knew Dina had received an outfit for today's event. She was an important person, so a slave was sent to get her ready. It was the opposite treatment of what Dina's lover had received after being captured.

Dina sat in a dark chamber. The young female slave had finished dressing her in a blue robe with silver decoration. Her shiny hair was beaded and braided, and she wore a silver belt with the Anubis symbol on the buckle and simple sandals. She turned to the doorway when she heard the high priest and the lower priests approaching her prison. Numerous footsteps echoed in the hallway, coming closer and closer. Two cymbal clangs in the hallway told her it was time for the dual execution.

Thutmose gestured for the other priests to wait outside. They would do as they were told because he was the highest-ranking priest in the whole of Egypt. He stepped inside the prison cell and motioned the slave to leave. She ran out quickly.

Dina fell to her knees when she saw her father in the high priest's outfit. "Please, father, help me! I don't want to die!"

Thutmose's face was distorted with emotion. "I can't help you, my daughter, in this life. But I can promise you revenge in the future."

Dina looked up at her father. "What should I do?"

"You must face your destiny for betraying your country, your pharaoh, and your gods." Her father looked distraught. Thutmose gestured to the guards by the doorway and commanded, "Take her to the execution site."

Two of the guards approached Dina and stood next to her.

She rose and glanced at her father. "I will do as you tell me to do."

Thutmose nodded, and they walked out and headed outside of the palace. The sun was bright and shone above them, the temperature scorching hot.

Thutmose commented, "Ra has blessed this day with his rays."

Dina replied, "My life is ending. I will pray for Apophis to kill this world as my world will soon be the world of the dead."

Thutmose paled. He knew his curse would allow Dina to do that.

3

The Slave's Execution

The crowd silenced and fell to the ground when the pharaoh's entourage arrived. He had only two hundred slaves accompanying him and sat on a golden throne carried by his favorite slaves. He wore the golden robe of the king, emblazoned with black images of the gods of Egypt. He had his blue *Khepresh* crown on. The snake was the king's insignia, a rearing cobra called the Uraeus, attached to the very front of the pharaoh's crown. It symbolized the protective goddess *Wadjet*.

The pharaoh's golden scepter had a stylized antelope head at its top. In his left hand, he carried a flail which was a rod with three strands of beads attached to the top, symbolizing a punishment.

Like most of his ancestors, he also had an *Ankh,* a cross with a teardrop-shaped loop on top, the symbol of life, hanging from a golden chain on his neck.

Thutmose kneeled and bowed his head as Pharaoh Akhenaten approached the riverside. Dina also kneeled, bowed, and raised her hands to Akhenaten. Her last plea was to save her life. "Please, my god of all Egypt, spare me. The slave seduced me. I didn't mean any harm to this land or your highness."

Pharaoh Akhenaten's gaze was icy. "No mercy. You violated the Gods of Egypt. You've heard your sentence." He turned his eyes to Thutmose and added, "Proceed with the sentencing."

Thutmose sighed. That was the final plea. Nothing could change the pharaoh's mind.

He turned to the guards. "Ready the slave."

Two guards approached and knelt beside Aper. He glanced up and swallowed hard; it was difficult to face his death. He was a slave, and he was worth nothing to these people. No one would help him. He turned his eyes to Dina and called to her, "Dina, my love, my god's gift. I will meet you in the afterlife."

Akhenaten's eyes turned angry, and he said, "No, you won't. Your head will be separated, and your limbs will be torn off your body. Your body parts will be scattered in the desert. No soul will find its way when it is torn apart."

Dina's face distorted in agony, and she shivered in fear. She had hoped to meet Aper in the other life, but the pharaoh squashed that hope. Her fear turned into anger towards the people of Egypt and the pharaoh who sentenced the lovers. She swore in her mind that she would get revenge for her lover and their lives as she cried out to Aper, "I love you. I will find you. I will bring your soul back to live with me."

Thutmose turned to the guards and nodded. Time to proceed with the execution. At the same moment, the guards lifted their swords cut off the slave's head, and then proceeded to hack off his limbs from his body. The crowd murmured as they watched the riverbank turn red from the blood of the slave. Thutmose heard someone say, "Now the crime has been punished. Hapi, the god of fishes, should be pleased. There will be plenty of fish on the river for us to catch."

The guards tied a rope to each limb, climbed on their horses, and waited for the pharaoh to sign that they could leave. Pharaoh Akhenaten lifted his flail and then lowered it, giving the sign to go. The guards rode toward the desert, pulling the body parts on a rope behind their horses. The dust cloud formed behind them, and soon, they were out of sight.

The sky was cerulean, and the desert sand gleamed golden in the sunshine. *A perfect day for anything except this horrible deed,* Thutmose thought. *How can any god forgive this day when I have to kill my flesh and blood?*

Dina glanced at his father, saw his distress, and sighed. She knew her turn was next.

She was still kneeling on the ground in front of the pharaoh. She kept her head bowed, as she didn't want to infuriate the pharaoh more than he was. The guards approached her and stood next to her, waiting for the entombing ceremony to start.

4

Dina, the God's Gift

Dina, I named you. Your name means God's gift. You were the god's gift to me, Thutmose thought as he glanced at his daughter kneeling on the ground.

The crowd fell silent. A warm breeze caressed Dina as she waited for the pharaoh to order her father to proceed.

Pharaoh Akhenaten surveyed the waiting crowd and the group of priests behind Thutmose, the high priest. His eyes met Thutmose, and he ordered, "It is time."

Thutmose nodded. He had no choice but to obey his god on Earth, the ruler of Egypt.

He turned to his lower priests and said, "Get my carriage. We'll take Dina to the tomb prepared for her. The lower priests performed menial tasks like opening doors, writing hieroglyph texts, butchering offering animals, and guiding new priest recruits whereas the higher-ranking priests were allowed to interpret the Gods' words, and signs, and predict future events. Only the high priest wielded so much power that he was practically a ruler in the land of Egypt because he had access to the Black Book of Anubis and the Golden Book of Ra which contained powerful incantations and spells.

One of the lower priests turned and soon returned with a black chariot led by two jet-black horses.

Thutmose said, "Guards, take the prisoner to the chariot."

The guards grabbed Dina by the arms, pulled her up, dragged her to the carriage, and pushed her to sit. They tied her arms to the sides of the carriage so she could not escape. The carriage was small, with room for only two people: the driver and the passenger. The other priests would follow the chariot on foot.

Thutmose climbed in next to her daughter and bowed to the pharaoh. "Your Highness, we are ready to go."

Pharaoh Akhenaten nodded. He would follow the priests to the tomb and wait outside. No one was allowed to enter the tomb, which would be cursed.

The somber entourage left the riverside and headed to the desert, with Thutmose leading the group in his black chariot. Their destination was near the Valley of the Kings.

Dina's tomb was a half-pyramid-shaped structure with one entrance. The heavy rocks were ready by the doorway, and no one would be able to open the tomb after the rocks were pulled over it.

It would be closed forever.

When Thutmose arrived at the scene, he pulled the horses to stop and then faced his daughter. "This will be your resting place for eternity. It's far away from the city and not in the Valley of the Kings. No one will come here. No one will hear your cries. You will die here cursed."

Large tears fell on Dina's cheeks as she nodded. Her throat felt tight, and she could not reply.

The lower priests opened the ties on her arms and let her climb down from the chariot. Then they strolled to the tomb.

Only Thutmose and his priests entered with Dina between them.

It was dark and smelled musty inside.

Two lower priests lit the torches on the walls before they continued to the large room in the middle of the structure. It was just an open space with no food or slaves for the afterlife.

Dina shivered. *This will be my last home, my last view of this world*, she thought.

Thutmose stopped in the middle of the floor. He opened the black book of *Anubis* and browsed it until he found his bookmarked page, the curse he planned to cite.

He faced Dina. "My daughter, my god's gift. It is time."

He gestured for the other priests to leave. The curse was not for their ears to hear.

The lower priests bowed, backed out of the room, and exited the tomb.

Now, Dina and her father were alone.

Thutmose explained the curse of the living dead. "Dina, this curse will allow you to return to earth and get your vengeance. You'll have the power to take lives and destroy the land. You can find your lover if you wish so."

"I will want all of that and more," Dina replied.

"Let me read the curse aloud, and Anubis will answer." Thutmose viewed the page he had chosen and then started his chanting. "Hail to you, my God, Anubis," he started. "Come, so that this woman born of my flesh will rise again."

He glanced at Dina, who shivered and crossed her arms in front of her.

"Come and listen to my words. Overturn the entombment, let the dead rise, and let Dina be the ruler of the living world. Let her be your hand. Let her hold your power. Let her get her revenge."

The tomb's air shimmered as the curse was finished. The room grew darker. The chattering of the scarab beetles quieted. A chilly breeze entered the tomb, and the hair on Dina's neck stood up. She trembled.

A shadow formed on the wall, growing larger. It had a head of a jackal.

Anubis had entered the tomb.

Dina held her breath.

Thutmose bowed. "My god Anubis. Please, grant my daughter her wish. She wants her revenge in the future. She'll die here but won't be dead because of you."

Anubis's shadow surrounded Dina like a veil and entered her mouth. She gagged but stood still.

When the shadow had disappeared, the room grew brighter, and the torches flickered.

"I must leave you to now. You have your sign from the god," Thutmose said and hugged his daughter for the last time.

When he exited the grave, the slaves were ready to push the stones to cover the doorway.

Thutmose ambled back to his chariot and climbed up. He watched the slaves finish their work, and then it was done. Her daughter had been buried alive but was cursed to live again.

When Dina's tomb was closed, the group left the area.

The tomb was forgotten.

No mention of it existed in any writing except for one papyrus Thutmose wrote the same evening retelling the story and what he had done. He left it for the future high priests to read. Only the high priests could know what he had done and what would become of his daughter, Dina, in the future: the destroyer of the worlds, the revenge incarnated, and the embodiment of Anubis's powers.

Woe to those who are alive when she returns, Thutmose thought as he rolled the papyrus and placed it among the secret rolls of the high priests.

5

The Tomb

Dina glanced around; only the torches flickered. Her heart beat faster. She was alone. This place would be her tomb.

She thought, *There must be some air flowing here because the fire would not flicker without an airflow.*

"Dina." A whisper echoed inside the tomb. The shadows moved and grew darker.

There is no one here with me, Dina thought. Who is talking? Am I imagining it?

Her breath hitched as she heard it again.

"Dina." It was a soft murmur coming right next to her ear.

Dina swallowed hard. She whirled around but saw nothing but shadows.

"Who is it?" she called out.

No one answered.

The lit area seemed to grow smaller even if the torches still burned just like they had before.

A man with the head of the jackal in the shadows! Dina glanced around and saw more shapes in the shadows. She saw the four-legged jackal shadows moving closer to the male figure. The chattering of the scarab beetles grew louder.

"Dina, your soul is mine," a hissing voice said.

"Who are you?" Dina whispered. No answer.

Dina tried to take a slow and deep breath in, but then she smelled the stench of decay in the tomb, not just the burning smell of torches.

"That is your body," the same voice whispered next to her ear. "I'll take your soul with me, and your body will stay here. The bones will be picked clean by my loyal beetles."

"You are Anubis!" Dina whispered.

Anubis was the god who guided the souls to the afterlife and weighed the heart and the soul to determine if they were worthy. He was the original god of the Dead before Osiris had taken the mantle from him, but Dina's father, Thutmose, believed Anubis had more power than what was generally considered. He had the black book of Anubis because he knew how powerful this god was. He had secretly collected more curses and prayers in the book than the lower-level priests could even imagine. Thutmose had read through many ancient manuscripts to find the most sinister and powerful curses and wrote them down in this book.

Thutmose knew Anubis would listen to the prays of the father, the high priest, when he needed help. Thutmose had read a curse from the book and offered Dina's soul in exchange for the favor from Anubis. Now it seemed that Dina had gotten what Thutmose had prayed for.

Dina heard the scarab beetles and saw them stop by the edge of the lit area where she stood. They are waiting for Anubis, the jackal-headed god, to stop talking and give them permission to eat me alive, she realized.

"Now, join me, Dina," the voice said, and the jackal-headed man entered the lit area and gestured to the scarabs. The black beetles scurried forward, climbing up her legs, and she felt bites digging inside her skin. She screamed, but no one could hear her pain and agony. Hundreds of beetles bit her and hung in her arms and legs, biting and chewing her skin, like needles stinging.

The jackals from the shadows joined the feast.

"This agony is your price. You'll receive what your father asked of me. Revenge in the future. You can give this same pain to the ones you wish to exact revenge upon," the voice whispered, and then he was gone.

A breeze came from nowhere and extinguished the torches. The room was pitch black. Dina's high-pitched screams echoed in the blackness until they finally stopped. Her soul was free and alive in the underworld, whereas her body had suffered a horrible death.

The torches were lit by an invisible hand again, revealing what had happened. The room was empty except for Dina's skeleton on the floor. All the skin, muscles, and organs had been picked and chewed. Her clean white bones were scattered on the stone floor. No signs of the jackals, the beetles, or the shadow figures.

The tomb was ominously quiet, waiting for the moment when someone would enter, and the cursed Dina would be free to roam in the new world.

Many hundreds of years passed, and Dina's tomb was lost in the past. Dina was forgotten. Her father's memoirs were lost as new pharaohs and priests rose to power. The Egyptian pharaoh's dynasty collapsed, and new rulers conquered the once mighty pharaoh's lands.

Dina's cursed tomb was covered in sand. Eventually, it was only one dune among thousands of others. If any traveler went by, they thought it was just another mound. They didn't know what lay beneath the sand and what was waiting to be awakened.

6

1940, Berlin

A man with a high forehead and short-cut hair stood in front of a large map depicting Egypt. He looked pensive. SS-Reichsführer Heinrich Himmler wore the signature black uniform, with shiny black boots, a traditional leather belt, and a crossbelt over his shoulder. His shirt collar was trimmed with a silver cord. He had the SS collar tabs of his rank in SS, an abbreviation of *Schutzstaffel* (in German: "Protective Echelon"). He had formidable power in the Third Reich leading the SS organization, which had morphed from a political bodyguard status to a feared paramilitary organization.

Heinrich Himmler was fascinated by ancient artifacts and their power, including the Holy Grail, the hammer of Thor, and the Holy Lance, the spear that pierced the side of Jesus. He believed these artifacts, if found, could be used as weapons by the Third Reich. He was not the only one in the Third Reich who longed to find supernatural treasures and religious relics. Adolf Hitler himself was interested in the occult and believed in magical powers.

Because of Himmler's status and the support of the Reichsführer, he had assigned several archeologists to investigate clues leading to ancient artifacts in different parts of the world, including Norway, North Africa, and from the Judaean Mountains to the Mediterranean area.

He had gathered a group of loyal SS officers in the room as he studied the map. He had recently received an ancient manuscript from an excavation in Egypt, where German archeologists had discovered an unknown tomb. They had not entered there yet, as they wanted to inform the headquarters of the Third Reich first in case there was something specific, they should be looking for inside the tomb.

"Could this have some ancient weapons from the pharaoh's time?" August Frank, the administrative officer, asked and leaned closer to view the map and the note the archeologist had sent them.

Curt von Gottenberg glanced at him and commented, "We don't know much about the ancient pharaohs and their weapons. We've heard of the cryptic curses the priests used. We could assume that there are treasures like gold, jewelry, and statues worth a fortune. That alone is a good reason to enter the tomb."

Heinrich Himmler stayed quiet and listened to the discussion in the room. He had already decided that the archeologist should enter the tomb. All the reasons his commanding officers had said were valid.

"It is my wish, and the wish of our leader, that we enter the tomb," Himmler stated with a quiet voice and glanced around to see if there were any objections. Every officer in the room stared at him and nodded. They all agreed. He was not a man to be crossed.

Himmler turned to his assistant, Werner Grothmann, and said, "Call the archeological camp and tell them to enter the tomb. We expect a full list of artifacts, valuables, and other items after they have been cataloged. Especially, ask them to look for books and manuscripts that could contain ancient curses and spells."

Werner clicked his heels, "Yes, Reichsführer." And he saluted by extending his right arm from the shoulder into the air with a straightened hand, the Sieg Heil salute, and left the room.

Werner Grothman had been wounded in June 1940 during the battle of France when Germany invaded France, Belgium, and Luxemburg, and after that, he was appointed to Himmler's staff. He had been his assistant since then and had earned Himmler's approval as a loyal Nazi officer, always ready regardless of the time of day, and accompanied Himmler on his field trips. He was a handsome young man in his mid-twenties, although his dark hair was already thinning on the top.

The meeting was over, and each officer greeted and left Heinrich Himmler alone. Werner knocked on the door when the last SS officers had left and said, "Reichsführer, I called the archeologists, and I talked with the leading archeologist and scholar, Walther Wolfe. He was excited about the excavation. He said that the preliminary findings placed the tomb around 1300 BC. He had studied the outside hieroglyphs and discovered that the tomb was secret. Inside was someone valuable to Thutmose, the high priest. Thutmose was in power under Pharaoh Akhenaten. He said the tomb looked like it had not been robbed. Wolfe believed that if the tomb is intact, as it seems, we can expect valuable items and treasure inside. Usually, this kind of tomb was reserved for high-ranking people, like pharaohs or their priests." Werner waited by the door to see if Himmler wanted to ask something else or if he had another task for him.

"Thank you, Werner, for letting me know. Let's hope Wolfe can find something worthy there," Himmler replied and gestured that Werner could go now.

Werner saluted and closed the door behind him, noting the Reichsführer's grim face and deciding not to ask questions because Himmler most likely had pressing state matters to deal with. *Reichsführer would call him if he needed assistance*, he thought.

Himmler viewed the map of Egypt again. The tomb was not in the Valley of the Kings but close by. He didn't expect it to be a pharaoh's tomb, but it could be a priest's tomb, just as Wolfe had suggested. He grabbed the map, rolled it to a scroll, placed it on the side of the table, and then walked to the window.

Adolf Hitler himself had ordered them to find religious artifacts, the more powerful, the better, but so far, his SS organization had not managed to do that. He sighed. He hoped he would not upset and disappoint the leader of the Third Reich and be replaced.

Perhaps, this new excavation in Egypt will bring some new treasure into light, Himmler thought. Then he turned and stared at the war map on the wall. The troops had conquered France, Belgium, and Luxembourg, and now the museums of those countries would be available for Nazi leaders to raid. He knew there were also Jewish artists in those museums, and he had given orders to destroy any paintings made by Jews. He wished to add some new German or French artists to his art collection, but he would let Hitler pick his paintings first.

His SS group had also been tasked with interrogating the prisoners and finding out the locations of enemy troops. He had decided to monitor the interviews himself in Paris the following week. *Busy week ahead*, he thought as he ambled to his desk, sat down, and started reading the latest reports.

7

1940, Egypt

Walther Wolfe, the chief German archeologist, had a neatly cut black beard and mustache. He wiped the sweat from his forehead. He was in a tent near a tomb they had discovered. He wore tan-colored slacks and a white shirt with sleeves rolled up to his elbows, but the hot and humid weather made the fabric feel stuck to his skin.

It was close to sunset time. No wind. The high dunes covered the view of the Valley of the Kings, which was located on the west bank of the Nile.

It was the area where the bodies of the pharaohs were laid to rest in tombs cut deep into the rock. These final resting places of the pharaohs range in size from single chamber burials to massive structures of many rooms.

The area where Walther had set up his camp was further away, but he could still see on the horizon the famous valley. His team had accidentally found this lost tomb. It had been buried, but the recent sandstorm had cleared the sand from the top, revealing it to the archeologist's keen eyes. Walther's team had been excited to find a new, unopened tomb that was not even mentioned in any documents they had read before. That was one reason they had contacted Himmler's office and informed him immediately because this could be an important discovery of Egyptian history.

Walther had a pipe on the table and reached out to light it, but he was interrupted by a servant, a young Egyptian boy at age ten. "Sahib! Message!"

He waved a paper in his hand. He had come from Cairo with the last group of traders who had brought more food and water to the camp.

Walther took the note from the boy and read it. "*Himmel, Arsch und Zwirn*!" He rushed out of his tent and walked to the neighboring tent. "Carl!"

A young blond-haired man in his thirties came from inside. "Ja?"

"The British archeologist team has arrived in Cairo. Our spy there reported that they are heading towards this area." Walther was red in the face.

"Calm down. You don't want to have a heart attack in this heat," his colleague Carl Manheim replied, then added, "They might be traveling in this direction, but they are more likely to go to the Valley of Kings. They could not have heard of our tomb. No one knows except us and Himmler's office, and we just talked with him yesterday. Himmler himself agreed that we could proceed and open the cave and look for either valuables or items with power." He put his hands in his pockets and added quietly, "The SS is a powerful organization. I don't think we'll have any trouble fighting off the Brits if they arrive here."

"Yes, you're right. I don't want to share my findings with them. We are here to prove the superiority of the Aryan race and the excellence of our archeological knowledge, and we will do that." Walther wiped his forehead again and added, "The sun will be setting soon. We should eat, and early tomorrow morning, we will remove the stones and break the tomb's seal."

"It will be interesting to see who is buried there and why," Carl said. "I didn't see any hieroglyphs outside to explain why this tomb was set alone here and who is inside."

"Yes, that was strange. I guess we'll get answers tomorrow," Walther replied. He turned and walked towards his own tent. "See you in ten minutes. We'll eat together."

"Jawohl," Carl replied and returned to his tent.

8

The Rivals

Walther Wolf held a horsehair fly whisk with a wooden handle in his hand to chase away the flying insects that bothered him in the tent. The dinner was kebab and rice with grapes for dessert. He poured red wine into glasses as his colleague Carl Manheim leaned back and lit a cigarette. It was one of those awful Egyptian brands that smelled bad and tasted even worse.

Walther sighed. He missed his German sausage and potato dishes with a pint of beer, but he hoped to return soon to Germany with a vast archeological treasure to please the head of the Third Reich. He even hoped to find an ancient book of spells that would be something special for the Nazi's top leaders.

The next morning, they would open the tomb.

He heard a ruckus outside the tent and went to see what was going on. The Brits had arrived! They had seen his camp and came by to check what he was doing there. Walther groaned when his eyes met the leader of the Brits group.

Sir Michael Merriweather was his worst rival! And there he was, waving happily at him as he sat on his camel.

"Walther! I didn't expect to see you here, old boy. What have you discovered?"

Sir Michael glanced eagerly at the ancient tomb dug out from under the sand, revealing a doorway blocked by heavy stones. He was a pudgy middle-aged man with large whiskers and wore a cotton shirt and slacks. He had a sun helmet and a similar whisk to swat away the flies that buzzed around the camel.

He's treacherous! He's going to take credit for this tomb, Walther thought and smiled sweetly at his enemy. "Well, isn't it, Sir Michael? How ever did you come to this part of the world? I thought you were still digging somewhere in Asia?"

"Ah, no, my dear friend, I finished that job a while ago, and I've been cataloging my recent findings. Then I heard rumors that a new tomb was found near the Valley of the Kings, and I just had to see it with my own eyes." He glanced toward the unopened tomb and added, "Is it this one?"

"Yes, of course, it is!" Walther grumbled. "It's mine, and you won't get any credit for finding it. I was here first and will record and report all my findings. It will all go to the Third Reich!"

Sir Michael twirled his long mustache between his fingers as if thinking, then added, "We'll stick around. You might need help."

"No, no, I don't need any help from you!" Walther said and gestured, shooing, his hand faced downward as he wiggled his four fingers to make the Brits leave.

"Really?" Sir Michael replied calmly and viewed the tomb again. "How do you plan to open that? Those massive stones require some manpower." He surveyed the German camp and added, "I don't see you having enough workers here to do that job."

Walther knew that. He didn't want to admit it, but his local workers had been slacking and disappearing from the site as if they didn't want to be there. He had only three men left of the twenty hired men he had two weeks before. None of the men had said anything; they simply disappeared one after another without any word. Only the slowest and the dumbest remained. They also looked like they didn't want to work there. He had wished many times that he could have German workers here. They would have a work ethic and finish the job they were hired for.

Walther's face turned red, and he opened his mouth, but Carl had come to stand next to him, and he put his hand on his arm and said quietly, "He is right, and you know it. We need help."

Walther took a deep breath and said, "Let's talk about the terms of this cooperation. Come to the dinner tent." He turned and marched back inside the tent.

Sir Michael and Carl followed him. Sir Michael brought with him another archeologist, Lewis Llewellyn. He was a young, slender man with thinning blond hair.

Carl opened a couple of folded chairs for their guests and offered some Turkish coffee.

Walther started the conversation. "I want it on the record that I was the first to find this tomb."

"Of course." Sir Michael nodded, sipped his coffee from a tiny cup, and then placed it on the table. "We'll share what's inside it."

"The Third Reich will have the first bids of the most valuable items," Walther added.

Sir Michael shook his head. "No, no, no. You must understand that if we lend you the manpower and the tools to open the tomb, we'll have some of the treasures. I'll say fifty-fifty."

Walther sighed.

Carl commented, "Our leaders want anything that has any spells on it. Anything to do with gods or occultism."

"Okay, we can agree on that. We're more interested in the sarcophagus and the traditional vases and sculptures. I'm sure we can work out the division of the items we find inside," Sir Michael replied. He glanced from Carl to Walther and asked, "Do we have a deal?"

"Yes! Yes, we do," Walther said.

No need to haggle because he knew Sir Michael would otherwise go and take his men with him. What would he do then? He'd have to go back to Cairo and find new men and lose more time and money; by then, someone might already have opened the tomb while he was gone.

No, this is a better deal, he thought.

"Swell! We'll camp close by and start tomorrow morning at dawn. Good night." Sir Michael got up, and his coworker Lewis followed him.

When they had left the tent, Walther wiped his forehead with his handkerchief and asked Carl, "Did I do right? I know we'll lose some items in this deal, but we don't have enough workers."

"Yes, I think that was a correct choice. We'll get the tomb open tomorrow," Carl replied and added, "I'll retire now. Good night and see you tomorrow."

"Good night!" Walther replied.

He remained seated in the dinner tent after everyone else had left. He wondered what they would see inside the tomb the next day. He hoped there would be a pile of jewels, valuable statues, and the usual plates, vases, and cups that were usually left full of food for the deceased so that he or she would not be hungry in the afterlife. *If this deceased was a wealthy person, then there could also be his slaves buried with him,* he thought.

9

The Excavation Site

Walther Wolf got up early. It was barely sunrise. He got dressed in his tropical cotton slacks, jacket with a white shirt, and brown leather travel shoes, then headed to the other tent for breakfast. He had wished for eggs over easy and bacon and some sausage, but the cook served cooked fava beans, pita bread, and boiled eggs with rice. *Not a breakfast for a German lad,* Walther thought, but his stomach was grumbling, so he picked up a plate, filled it, and then took a cup of strong coffee.

His associate Carl entered the tent when Walther had almost finished his breakfast. “Good morning, Walther. You are early this morning!”

Carl tossed his white Fedora hat on the side table, then walked to where the cook had placed the container with food and a pile of utensils and plates ready. He took a fork, a knife, and an empty plate while checking out the hot dishes.

“Yes, I want to be ready to open the tomb. If I’m not there early, the Brits will go and smash the doorway down without waiting for us.” Walther sipped his strong black Turkish coffee while waiting for Carl to finish his breakfast. “We should go there when you’re done with your breakfast. By the way, the beans were good this morning. Not hard like last time,” Walther added.

“Oh, good. I was afraid they’d be undercooked again.” Carl turned and went back to put another scoop of beans on his plate.

Carl wore simple tan slacks and a white long-sleeve shirt with sleeves rolled up to his elbows. Even this early in the morning, the humidity was high, and the day promised to be scorching hot.

After fifteen minutes, the German archeologists were ready to start the most important day of their archeological excavation so far: the opening of the tomb they had found.

The Brits had set up their camp higher up, and as the Germans walked to the tomb to view it one more time, a group of people left from the Brit’s camp heading their way.

“Ahoy, Walther! Wait for us,” Sir Michael Merriweather called him.

Walther grimaced. He hated to cooperate with his adversary, but he had no choice. "Good morning, Sir Michael. I hope you had a pleasant night," he replied and waited for Sir Michael to come closer.

"Yes, I slept like a baby. The treasures of that tomb were filling my dreams," Sir Michael replied, chuckling. He had his tropical sun hat on with a neck flap and a cane in his hand. He pointed his cane toward the half-uncovered tomb's opening and said, "My crew is ready, they will start digging the rest of the sand away from the doorway, and then we can examine how to open it without collapsing the whole structure."

Sir Michael must have noticed the teeth grinding and a sour look on Walther's face because he added, "Don't worry, Walther. We'll both get famous with this excavation. It's the find of the decade. I'll promise you that."

"Yes, I'm sure it is," Walther muttered. He shoved his hands in his front pockets and watched as the Brits' team marched forward with their shovels and started digging the sand and shoveling it away from the opening area. He knew Sir Walther was correct in his assumption: this tomb was an important discovery, and he couldn't have managed to open it by himself with the few local servants he had left.

The view of the locals digging the sand made him think again, why did his servants leave without notice? They had disappeared in the middle of the night. He had checked the camp, and they had left without a trace. Did they know something about this tomb that he and the Brits didn't know?

"Sir Michael," he started, "Do you think a curse is involved with this tomb?"

Sir Michael glanced at Walther curiously. "Usually, we hear the normal rumors of curses to those who open the pharaoh's resting places. I don't believe this is a pharaoh's tomb. It's not located in the Valley of the Kings, where the pharaohs are buried. This is built far away from the valley, and I have not found any ancient documents to describe who could be buried here and why." He studied Walther's face and asked, "Why do you ask? Do you know something?"

Walther quickly shook his head. "No, I was thinking of our local servants who disappeared. Why did they leave so suddenly? We pay them well, better than they would get in other jobs in Cairo."

"True. They might have feared the rumors of curses." Sir Michael turned to face the excavation again. The job was progressing quickly, and they would have the tomb's doorway open soon

Walther wiped the sweat from his forehead with a handkerchief. "Your team is doing a great job. We can examine the doorway and the surrounding walls in another hour or so."

Sir Michael glanced at him and nodded. He was pleased with his team too. "Yes, they are efficient. Let's go closer to have a look at the wall. Perhaps, we can even see engravings of your curse on the wall or the doorway."

He chuckled as he noted Walther's face turning red. He didn't wait for Walther's answer but gestured for his colleagues to follow him. They met Sir Michael's young colleague there supervising the excavation. Lewis Llewellyn turned to greet them when they arrived at the site.

"We're almost ready to check out the walls and the doorway. A few more minutes," Lewis announced excitedly.

Sir Michael stood at the edge of the excavation area, and Walther and Carl followed him there. The tomb's doorway area was right below them. It was clear the tomb had been buried deep in the sand. No one had gone inside for centuries.

10

The Tomb

The stone walls of the tomb were cleared, and the archeologist group walked next to the tomb to inspect the walls more thoroughly.

Walther grimaced as he saw the revealed hieroglyphs winding around the doorway, which was still closed. "This mentions a curse."

Sir Michael put on his metal-framed glasses and nodded. "Yes, it does mention that. It says: Whoever enters this tomb will release the evil onto the earth. Anubis protects the one whose remains are inside, and the buried one will rise when the first rays of sunshine hit the chamber." He moved forward to read the other side of the doorway. "The curse in this tomb is so horrible that no man has ever faced it. The ones who open the door will face the death of the most hideous kind."

"Ah, that doesn't sound pleasant. Are you sure you translated it correctly?" Walther asked and moved to read it himself. "Yes, it seems so."

"It does not mention who is buried inside," Carl commented.

"All the major tombs have had a curse written. They all warn not to disturb the resting place of the buried ones. I don't believe this is any different," Sir Michael said. "Let's figure out how to open the door."

"It seems as if the solid block of stone has been pushed tight against the doorway, so no one can move it from inside. It will need a stick of dynamite to blast it open, which I prefer not to use in a discovery like this, or we need more men to hoist the block away from the doorway."

"We could heat the rock then cool it. The mud in between the rocks would crumble, and then we can use the battering ram to pound away the stone blocking the entrance," Carl suggested.

"That sounds good. We don't have a battering ram, but I'm sure our staff can make one soon enough," Sir Michael replied. "Your suggestion is better than blasting away the doorway."

Some of the local helpers got the fire going and heated the doorway area with it, while others had vinegar ready to cool it down. They continued doing this for a few hours.

It took them a good part of the morning to build a decent battering ram, but when it was finally finished, the local helpers placed it in the front of the doorway. The heating and cooling of the stone and the mud in between the rocks had helped as they examined the mud crumbling. Even some of the stones had cracked after heating and cooling.

"Let's get on with the ram next!" Sir Michael ordered. The local helpers gathered around the ram. They wore their typical kaftan robes, which were cool in the hot heat of the day.

A couple of workers hesitated to start breaking down the doorway. They seemed to know what the hieroglyphs said as they murmured to each other.

"What's going on down there?" Lewis called them. "We need to get this doorway open before the sunset. We want to see what's inside."

"Yes, Mr. Lewis," one replied, bowing to him. He pointed at the couple who had exchanged words with each other and added, "The locals say an evil curse is upon the people who open this tomb, and they are afraid to open this."

"Tell them that all the tombs have the same warning, and nothing has happened to those who opened the other tombs before this one," Lewis replied. He walked back to the edge of the excavation to watch the opening with the other archeologists.

The ram hit the doorway with a loud boom. With each strike, the stone shattered a bit more, and then eventually, the stone covering the doorway cracked, leaving it partly open.

A cloud of fine dust wafted out from the opening of the tomb. It formed a shape of a snake with its fanged mouth open and hit the nearest local worker on the neck. He screamed and fell to the ground. His neck had two small red dots like a snake bite. He was dead in seconds.

The smoke curled in the air lowered to the ground and transformed into a shape of an alligator. With swift moves, it opened its mouth, grabbed the next victim by the leg, and bit it off. The local worker screamed as his blood sputtered from the bit off his leg.

The next worker faced an angry cloud of bees which covered him, and he fell to the ground, swollen from bee stings and not breathing.

The remaining workers ran away and started climbing up the hill to the edge of the excavation, trying to escape the killing smoke.

The smoke curled and changed its shape to a rope, and it strangled the next victim, who collapsed with his neck distorted and bruised.

"This is not possible!" Sir Michael muttered. "There is a curse in this tomb."

"It's killing all the workers who opened it," Carl added.

"Are we safe?" Walther asked, taking a few steps backward.

"I'm not sure. The curse said anyone who opens. We didn't open it, but we were present when it was opened," Sir Michael commented. "I don't know how precise the curse is, but I would not stay here and wait for the smoke to find us. We can come back later when it's dissipated."

11

The Next Steps

The archeologists quickly ran towards the camp when the smoke approached the excavation's edges. They stopped halfway between the camp and the excavation. They could still see the tomb's opening and observe what was happening.

"I think the smoke is dissipating now," Walther said, glancing back to the site.

Running on dunes was difficult because every step sank into the sand, and it was hard to balance. Walther sat down on the sand and huffed and puffed as he pulled out his big white handkerchief and wiped the sweat off his red face.

Carl stopped next to him and cautiously surveyed the excavation site peppered with the dead bodies of their labor workers. “Sir Michael, I think you lost most of your workers in that incident.”

Sir Michael took deep breaths to calm down his breathing after running away from the site like the others and replied, “Yes, it seems there was a curse. It only hit the ones who opened the tomb. The smoke evaporated after the last one of the workers who used the ram was killed. I think we are safe.”

Lewis looked suspicious. “We don’t know if there are more curses inside that tomb.”

Sir Michael waved his hand. “No, I don’t believe there are. The doorway did not mention anything like that. None of the other tombs excavated in Egypt have had several curses.” He turned his blue eyes to the excavation site, and his eyes gleamed with greed. “I’m sure we’ll be able to go inside safely. Nothing to worry about, my dear Lewis.”

Carl pulled Walther up from the ground. “Do you still want to proceed inside the tomb?” he asked quietly so that only Walther heard his question.

Walther only pondered it for a few seconds before answering. “We must go inside. The Third Reich would consider leaving this site to Brits as treason. They would immediately put us in front of the firing squad when returning to Berlin with no treasures, having given this up to the enemy archeologists." He shook his head sadly and added, "Dear boy, we have no choice but to go inside."

Walther brushed the sand off his slacks and then straightened. He viewed the tomb; it looked calm. The stone that had covered the doorway had been split and cracked, and you could see a small crevice leading inside. He couldn't see what was in there. His archaeological curiosity piqued, he pointed at the opening and asked, "We could go remove the rest of the stone that blocked the opening. I think it would be safe to do now."

Sir. Michael had taken out his cigarette and smoked it casually while watching the tomb. "Hm, I think I agree with you. Anyone who removes the rest of the stone that covers the doorway is not opening it. It is already open, so the curse will not affect you." He glanced at his colleagues and added, "Who would be brave enough to do that? All the workers down there are dead. We'd have to get more from Cairo."

"That would be wise. We could hide the bodies of these men before the next ones come, and they would not know anything that happened to them," Lewis commented. "We'll have a few servants left in both camps. Perhaps if we pay them a bonus, they will help clean up the site."

"Good idea. I can send a telegram to Cairo and ask for more labor," Sir Michael said. "Let's proceed if no one else has other suggestions."

Walther shrugged. "No, I think it is a wise idea to get rid of the bodies before the next crew sees them." He turned away and added, "Come and get me when you get the new crew here. I'll be in my tent. Come, Carl."

Carl followed him back to the German camp.

"Am I completely wrong, or is it unwise to enter the tomb?" Carl asked when they were out of hearing distance.

Walther nodded. "I think we should proceed with caution. There could be deadly traps or surfaces covered with poison. The Egyptians were clever. If there is something valuable inside the tomb, they have taken precautions to protect it even after closing it."

"Do you believe the poisons will still work after so many centuries?" Carl asked, opening the flap that closed Walther's tent.

"The opening curse seemed to work, so yes, I believe whatever they have inside will be functional, too," Walther replied and went inside his tent. "Come with me. Let's have a drink. We have time to kill."

Bad choice of words, Carl thought as he remembered the recent deaths of the local workers, but he followed the senior archaeologist to his tent.

12

The New Crew

The new crew needed some extra incentives to go near the excavation. They didn't understand what had happened. The new crew leader asked Sir Michael, "How were all the workers killed? What killed them?"

Sir Michael leaned on his cane and looked calmly at the new local worker. "It seems that the air in the tomb was toxic. When the stone cracked, the poisonous air drifted out, and the ones close to the opening inhaled it and died." He pointed to the tomb and added, "No need to worry. The air is clean now. We are standing here and talking, and nothing has happened to us."

The local leader, Achim, was a skinny man whose robe hung loose on his bony body. He had worn leather sandals on his feet and a red fez on his head. He bowed and backed away to talk to his crew of six men. They chatted eagerly with each other, and then Achim returned. "Yes, we will help to clean the bodies away. It's bad luck to leave them there out in the open, and it will attract wild animals to this site. No good. We need extra pay."

Sir Michael nodded. Lewis came closer with a bag of coins with him. He handed them to Achim and said, "Here, divide these coins with your team. They are yours if you get rid of the bodies in two hours."

Achim bowed but deeper this time and hurried back to show his crew how much extra payment they had received from the archeologists.

"Let's go talk with our German colleagues," Sir Michael said and headed to the German camp. When he reached Walther's tent, he called out, "Walther, the bodies will be cleaned up in two hours. We can continue our work then."

"Come inside, Sir Michael," Walther called from inside the tent.

"It's too hot to wait for two hours outside. Let's have a drink and a snack while we wait," Walther suggested.

Carl took the hint and went to look for their cook, and in less than fifteen minutes, he returned with a plate full of avocado and chicken stuffed croissants, butter cookies, and hot Turkish coffee.

"Ah, that looks great," Sir Michael commented when Carl walked inside.

While they had their snack, Achim's crew collected the bodies into a cart and pulled them away. Six dead bodies. The smoke in the form of a rope had killed three altogether. The snake had killed one, and the alligator-shaped smoke another one.

When two hours had passed, Achim walked to the German camp and looked for Sir Michael. He found him inside Walther's tent. "It's done. All the bodies have been removed, and we buried them in a shallow grave further away," Achim informed him.

"Well done. Let's go check out our tomb," Sir Michael said to the other archeologists, who all got ready to go out with him.

Carl picked up his camera with him to photograph the discovery and their progress.

Each archeologist grabbed a canteen bottle of water before leaving the tent's shade. The German servant had made them ready earlier that morning, knowing that the team would need plenty of water while digging at the tomb site.

The sand glittered in the sun as they stepped outside and headed to the excavation site. It was eerily quiet.

The four archeologists stopped by the edge of the excavation site. Everything looked calm. No bodies were in sight, just as Achim had promised. The tomb looked innocently calm and waiting for them.

Sir Michael gestured at others to follow him, and he walked down the excavation site. The wooden ladders had been built to help the climbing down because the sand was treacherous, and you could easily fall. Besides, the wooden structures around the tomb's opening kept most of the dug and piled sand out of the way.

When they reached the site level, they stopped and studied the tomb's doorway.

"When do we get the new workers?" Walther asked.

Lewis replied, "I sent a message to Cairo with my radio. They are on their way. I believe they should be here in a couple of hours if they left immediately."

"Good." Walther turned to Sir Michael and asked, "Do you want to wait for the crew? If not, we can start inspecting the tomb's walls and the doorway area. Some hieroglyphs need to be copied and photographed."

"That sounds good. If you take the left side, we can take care of the right side of the tomb," Sir Michael suggested. And they proceeded to view the walls.

The tools of the trade, the little brushes, shovels, and picks, were left on site earlier, so they didn't need to look for them. With immense care, both teams of archeologists surveyed the stone walls, and Carl took pictures of both sides of the tomb whenever one of the other archeologists called him to do that.

Two hours went fast, and they took breaks to sip water as the sun was hot and it was important to keep hydrated in the heat.

They heard a commotion coming closer and saw a camel caravan approaching.

"Ten camels! No, maybe fifteen," Lewis said as he stared at the distance. The caravan came closer, he recognized them, and he took off his brim hat and waved with a hat in his hand to get their attention. "It's our men from Cairo with new workers! They are here."

"Good timing!" Sir Michael said and turned to see the approaching group. "We just finished analyzing and capturing the outside hieroglyphs, and Carl has many fine photographs of the exterior walls now."

Walther nodded. "Yes, Carl is excellent at photographing. You won't be disappointed in his work."

"Let's greet our new workers. They will need to carry away the rest of the stone blocks from the doorway," Sir Michael said and waited for the caravan to stop.

"Achim can lead them. He did well with the bodies," Lewis suggested.

"It might be better to keep this group away from the others. If they hear about the dead bodies, they might not want to work," Sir Michael replied.

"The new workers can stay near our camp, so they won't have a chance to discuss with Achim and his team," Walther suggested.

"Yes, that's a great idea. Let's tell them that. Lewis, go up and point out where they can camp, and return here when you're done. The men can come here and start moving the stones when they are ready." Sir Michael turned his back on the caravan and viewed the tomb again.

It is hard to believe that this tomb has already caused six men's deaths. It looks so harmless. Just a pile of stones in the middle of the desert, Sir Michael thought. Aloud he said, "I'll go sit in the shade. The midday sun is too hot for me."

"We'll join you," Walther replied and gestured for Carl to come with them.

A canvas tent was on the site, and they went inside it. It had two simple tables with wooden folding chairs leaning against them. Not a luxury place, but suitable for resting while waiting for the excavation to continue with a new team.

Carl wiped off the sand and dust from the folding chairs, opened them, placed them on the floor near the table, and then let the senior archeologists sit before he followed their example. Walther sighed and wiped off the sweat with a handkerchief. "How can it be this hot all the time?"

Sir Michael laughed. "The weather here is nothing like in England or Berlin. It's always hot, humid, and dry. We don't get this much sunshine in England during the whole summertime."

"Yes, you're right. I wish I could sometimes excavate in a cooler climate with decent food," Walther replied. "Northern Europe would suit me well."

"Ah, yes. That would be something, but I don't think our generation is interested in anything we could discover there. No ancient artifacts to find or centuries-old tombs," Sir Michael replied.

When they heard rapid talk in Arabic outside the tent, Carl stood up and glanced through the tent's opening. "The crew is here. We can start."

13

Inside

Walther waged an unceasing war against the dust and brushed away the sand that had accumulated on his shoes and slacks while inside the tent.

Carl smiled. He knew Walther liked to be properly dressed, and this eternal sand was something he hated. He loved the charm of the ancient pyramids and the dunes that reached miles and miles as far as you could see. It was so different from Germany. *Like the fairytale of a thousand and one nights*, he thought.

The scorching sun poured down when they stepped outside and greeted the new crew. Their leader was an elderly man, Husan. He had a blue *litham*, a face veil, which protected him from the heat and dust and covered his head. He opened it to greet the archeologist. His face was narrow, he had sharp black eyes and a dark beard, and he wore a colorful cotton *galibya* robe.

His eyes latched on Sir Michael, and Walther bowed and waited for instructions. Carl came outside after the two senior archeologists. "Sir Michael? We received your message. I've brought ten men with us to help in this excavation." He glanced around and frowned. "I thought you had more men here."

"They disappeared," Sir Michael said. "An unforeseen event which totally disorganized our schedule here."

Lewis pointed to the entrance of the tomb. "I'm glad you came so fast. We really could use extra hands to pull out the rest of the stones from the tomb's doorway so we can go inside."

"Yes, sir. We'll get to it right away," Husan replied and gestured to his men, spoke some orders rapidly in Arabic, and gestured to the doorway.

The men in similar robes took the large rods, chisel hammers, and shovels that the previous crew had left behind and started working on the doorway. They carried away the smaller pieces of rock, then proceeded to move the larger parts of the stone still covering the entrance. They shoved the rods under the stone and used their muscles to push them aside. It didn't take them more than half an hour before the doorway was cleared.

Walther and Carl viewed the process on the edge of the excavation. They had climbed up there because they didn't want to get caught in another puff of curse smoke.

Walther rubbed his chin with his fingers. He stared at the tomb as if waiting for something evil to happen.

Carl was busy studying his map, then another one which contained the stars in the sky. "Walther, this tomb is aligned with Orion's Belt."

"The Ancient Egyptians knew their stars," Walther replied as he viewed the maps in Carl's hand.

Sir Michael and Lewis had stayed behind and waited by the tent. It was still further away from the tomb's entrance, so they believed they were safe. Sir Michael twisted his long mustache between his fingers, as he always did when thinking something or occupied in deep thoughts. This time though, he watched keenly to see if any men showed any signs of curse or being ill. Nothing happened. Everything looked fine. He almost believed himself now that the cursed smoke had not happened and that it had all been his imagination. *It must have just been poisoned air that bloomed out when the entrance stone was cracked*, he thought.

He gestured with his hand to Walther and Carl. "Let's go! The doorway is open. We can go inside." He turned and gazed at the tomb thoughtfully. *What treasures are you hiding? Who is buried there?*

Walther and Carl climbed down the wooden stairs and approached the British archeologists.

The four archeologists stopped by the doorway. The air smelled dry and dusty inside the tomb, but they didn't detect anything foul. It was like any other tomb they had visited in the Valley of the Kings, except this was not a pyramid. They had no idea who was buried in this tomb.

The earliest hieroglyphs inside the pyramid chambers are from around 3500 BC, Sir Walther thought as he lit the torch and held it high when they walked down the hallway. *These walls are covered with images. This must be a newer tomb.*

Carl grabbed Walther's arm and stopped him. He showed his compass. It was going around wildly. "The compass doesn't work inside. There must be something magnetic that interferes with it."

"Interesting," Walther muttered. "It has to be inside the walls because I don't see anything here." He inspected the walls again with the light of his torch.

The walls were covered with drawings of Anubis, the jackal-headed deity, receiving gifts from Egyptians. *Not hieroglyphs*, Walther thought.

Sir Michael had gone first with Lewis, and they reached the end of the narrow hallway leading to the burial chamber. They stopped in surprise. "No coffins or mummies here!" Sir Michael called back to Walther.

"Why was this place built if not to bury someone?" Walther asked, taking brisk steps to reach the entrance to the chamber.

"Ah, I didn't say that. There is a body, or a pile of bones, actually." Sir Michael pointed at the floor.

He was right. When Walther glanced at the floor towards the spot Sir Michael pointed, he saw the same thing. Someone had died here, but whoever it was, this person had not been buried properly like the Egyptians usually did. This one had not been prepared for the afterlife.

"How odd," Walther said.

As he stepped into the chamber to study the bones, the floor disappeared under him, and he fell into a deep abyss. His cries echoed and then stopped to a thump. All went quiet.

"Walther, are you okay?" Sir Michael called after him and looked down on the hole where Walther had fallen in.

No sound.

A slight breeze came from nowhere and brushed the archeologists. "You are mine," a quiet voice whispered in Arabic.

"Who is that?" Carl looked around, holding his lit torch up. The shadows grew larger, and the torchlight didn't seem to light the room as it had before. The torch seemed to burn less brightly.

A fire can't dim, Carl thought, frowning.

"It can die just like you," someone whispered in his ear, and when he turned around, he felt a sting on his leg.

He glanced down and saw a cobra curling around his ankles. *It bit me! One of the most poisonous snakes in the world.*

Sir Michael dropped his cane, backed away from the chamber, turned around, and ran outside. *This place is cursed!*

Lewis started to back up, but then he heard the soft voice whispering, "You'll give me a new body."

He frowned. *What does that mean? Who is talking?* He held his torch in his left hand and took out his pistol. No more snakes on the floor, he checked. He took a few steps back, and then he felt a slight touch like a soft hand caressing his cheek and brushing his hair.

He turned around, and it was the last thing he did. A swift cloud of smoke entered his nose and mouth, and he gagged and tumbled down. His eyes turned glassy, and his body contorted.

"Mine!" the voice repeated, but now the voice came inside Lewis's body. His body stopped moving, and he blinked rapidly. His irises turned from blue to black. He inhaled deeply, sat up glancing at his arms and hands, and wiggled his fingers.

"It is so strange to have a body again," the voice said to herself. "I was never a man, but this body will do until I find a more suitable one." He stood up and picked up the torch from the floor. "Come to me, my pets," he said, and the scuttle of tiny steps echoed in the chamber, and hundreds of black beetles came forward and stopped on Lewis's feet. "Go out and destroy!"

The floor seemed to move as the black army of beetles rushed to the hallway and outside. They burrowed under the sand, so the workers didn't see them, then attacked. One after another, the workers cried in pain and fell to the ground.

Lewis walked slowly out of the tomb. Sir Michael had climbed up on the wooden steps to the edge of the excavation site. He glanced back when he heard the cries of his workers.

The curse! The tomb is cursed! It's killing everyone! he thought, panicked, but then he saw Lewis appear unharmed from the tomb. *How odd*; *Lewis is alive.* That was his final thought because the beetles reached him, and he fell backward into the excavation with the beetles covering his body.

Lewis stopped by the entrance. He glanced at the bright sun and the dunes. "It's been centuries since I saw the sun and felt its rays on my face," he said to himself.

14

Anubis

Dina had taken the body of Lewis Llewellyn, a young, slender archeologist working for the British Museum. She knew nothing of this new world she had entered and stood by the entrance, not knowing what to do or where to go. Then she saw a movement from the corner of her eye, and she turned to see one of the jackal-headed carvings on the wall moving. The figure stepped out of the wall and grew taller than Dina, staying in the shadow of the entrance while Dina stood blocking the sunrays of the outside world.

The jackal-headed god, Anubis, was here, Dina thought, scared. The god wore a blue headpiece and golden knee-length loincloth. On his head, the god wore a blue *nemes,* a headpiece covering the whole head with lappets hanging in front of both shoulders and wide golden bracelets on his wrists.

The jackal-headed figure spoke to Dina with a booming voice. "The time of your revenge on the pharaoh and his world is now. Use it well. You have only seventy-two hours to be in that body you chose."

Dina frowned. She had not known there was a limit to the curse. "What will happen after seventy-two hours?"

"You'll return to the kingdom of Death unless you have the golden heart scarab. Wear that, and you can live forever," the jackal's harsh voice replied, and the figure returned to the wall.

"Wait! I don't know what that looks like," Dina said.

The wall in front of her transformed, showing an image of a golden scarab beetle with two shiny obsidian stones as eyes. The beetle looked alive.

It's a heart stone shaped like a scarab, Dina realized. She remembered the heart stones. They silenced the heart in the afterlife when Anubis weighed the worth of the deceased, so the heart could not tell lies or shameful tales against the deceased, and thus, the deceased could show how valuable his life had been and that he was worthy of achieving an afterlife.

In my case, I must show my worthiness in this life, to live forever, Dina thought, grimacing. *That's the reason for the scarab heart stone.*

"Your father, Thutmose, became the ruler after Akhenaten died. He wore the scarab beetle in his crowning ceremony as the regent of the land. He was not the pharaoh but ruled instead of the child pharaoh. His time was short, though. He was killed five years into his reign by a cult dedicated solely to Ra."

Nice to learn what happened to my father, but I still don't know how to find that heart scarab, Dina thought. "How do I find this scarab?"

A menacing laugh echoed in the now-empty tomb. "That is your task, not mine to tell you. You have seventy-two hours. If you fail, you will return to my kingdom and spend eternity in the pool of dead, not living but constantly dying."

Dina shivered and paled. That future did not sound appealing at all.

The jackal-headed figure vanished back to the wall and turned into one of the carved and painted figures on the wall.

Dina inhaled quickly and stood still while the god disappeared.

The tomb was silent again.

Dina touched the wall where the jackal-headed god was, but the stone wall was cold, and the figure was still. *The god Anubis was gone, returned to his world*, she thought.

She glanced at her hands. They were not female hands like she had used to. She was in a man's body. She didn't know anything about this world. She didn't even know how many decades or centuries had passed.

Dina assessed her clothing: long slacks, leather shoes, and a white shirt which all felt strange. She was used to linen and cotton dresses decorated with beads. She touched her head: thinning and short hair. She missed her long black locks. Could she switch a body to a woman's body while there was time, or would she have to stay like this?

First, she should find out who this man was and whose body she now possessed. Perhaps, there were clues outside. She saw tents and ladders leading upwards from the excavation.

Time to find the scarab, she thought and left the tomb.

15

Dina

When Dina, disguised as Lewis Llewellyn, walked away from the excavation site, which was now deserted because of her little beetle pets, her shadow cast behind her revealed her true form: the shapely figure of a young woman with the head of a jackal.

She left behind the bones of the workers as well as the archeologists. *The bones are clean, and soon the sand will bury them,* she thought.

"Come to me, my little pets. It's time to go," she called to her black beetles, which scurried after her. They climbed up her shoes, into her pant legs, and disappeared under the clothing.

In the distance, she saw tents, which she figured were where this man or the other her pets had killed stayed.

Dina marched across the dunes. The landscape looked like it had back then, but the tents looked different, and so were the tools back at the excavation site, she thought.

She went to the German camp and entered the tent with the cook, where the meal was ready. She glanced around, and when she saw the cook, she addressed him. "Servant, bring me a meal and explain my duties here."

"*Es tut uns leid...*" The cook looked surprised. First, he didn't understand the man in front of him because he had not spoken in German or English but in some ancient version of the ancient Egyptian language.

Dina realized her own mistake and pointed at the table.

The cook nodded and gestured that the visitor could sit down.

"How do I communicate with you if I don't know your language?" Dina muttered, glancing at the served food. She recognized meat and rice. She tried a little bit of each but realized she did not need any food. "I need to find someone who can speak for me and who understands me, and it's not you."

Dina shook her sleeves, and dozens of black beetles rushed out and attacked the cook eating him alive. Ten minutes later, his bones were bare, and Dina left the tent, gathering her pets.

The next tent was the German archeologists' tent. Dina browsed around and recognized familiar images of the River Nile, the Valley of the Kings, and the pyramids. The language was strange in the books, so she tossed them on the floor.

Time to go check out the next camp, she thought. The other camp was further away. She looked like Sir Michael's assistant Lewis Llewellyn when she walked across the dunes but she didn't know him and didn't have his skills or thoughts even if she had taken his body.

The campsite was empty, and the tents were similar to the other camp.

She viewed the table, the documents, the papyrus, and the books. Nothing in her language, she noticed with disappointment. *How can I find the golden heart scarab? I don't speak the language of the people I have met.*

Dina was about to leave when she heard a sound. A noise of something she had never heard before. She went outside and saw a square metal carriage approaching the camp faster than a camel could run. A cloud of dust appeared behind it.

What a strange thing that is! I guess it is a carriage of some sort, but it does not have camels or horses in front, Dina wondered and stopped by the tent's opening and waited for the monstrous carriage to come closer. She saw that there were two people inside it.

"Hello! We came to help you with the tomb findings!" the man yelled.

Dina didn't reply. Her eyes were fixed on the other person. She was a beautiful young female with long dark hair and an oval face. *She is perfect!* Dina thought. *I could live in her body forever.*

The strange carriage stopped next to the tent, and a man jumped off and then helped the young woman down. "I'm Jack Stiller, and this is my sister Lillian Stiller. She is the archeologist and the ancient language specialist in our family."

Dina didn't understand a word Jack had said, but she stared at the woman. She asked in the ancient Egyptian language, "Do you speak my language?"

"Yes," the woman replied in the same language.

"Perfect. Then I have some use for you," Dina replied. "Perhaps this other one can serve us too. I let you both live." She had thought about taking Lillian's body, but she needed a translator in this new world. She could find some other woman later.

Jack could only understand a few words of what Dina said and glanced curiously at Lillian, who had paled. Lillian asked in an ancient language, "What do you mean? Who are you?"

"I'm the one who was in the tomb. I took this body temporarily. I need help finding a heart scarab," Dina explained.

"Where are the other archeologists?" Lillian asked and took a few steps backward.

"Dead, of course," Dina replied.

"Who are you?"

"Dina."

16

The Search for the Heart Scarab Starts

Lillian's stomach clenched, and her heart tripped for several beats when she heard the answer that the other archeologists were dead. She translated that to Jack.

This person in front of me must know the reason, Lillian thought. Unless... she is the reason! Who is Dina? I've never heard of anyone by that name.

While Jack couldn't' understand much of the ancient language, he had recognized the word dead.

Jack, her brother, quickly glanced around. He didn't see anyone else at the camp. No signs of life anywhere. "Are you joking, Lillian? You must have misunderstood this man. How can everyone be dead? We just spoke with Sir Michael yesterday!"

Dina's black eyes locked on his blue ones as she replied coldly. "I'm your new master, your pharaoh. Follow me, and I might spare your life."

Jack glanced at Lillian, who quickly translated. He replied angrily, "No, I'm not a slave. There are no pharaohs. You're delusional, lady!"

Dina looked at Jack pitying and replied hissing, "Yes, you are, you little maggot of this new world. You either serve me or die!"

She held out her hand, lifted her fingers upwards, and muttered something. A swirl of sand appeared under Jack's feet. He started sinking downwards to a sandpit that seemed to consist of quicksand. He sank to his waist in seconds. Lillian cried and kneeled next to him. She grabbed his hands and tried to pull him up, but he was sinking fast, and the pull of the sand was too strong.

Realizing it was Dina's doing, she bowed her head and spoke in her language, "Please, he is my brother. We will both serve you loyally if you let him go."

Dina lifted her hand with her fingers upwards and mumbled something. The sand stopped swirling, and Jack stood in a sandpit sunk up to his armpits. "Help me up, Lillian!"

Lillian tried to pull him up, but he was too heavy. "I can't."

She glanced at Dina and requested, "Please, help him."

Dina stood still. "He has not agreed to serve me."

Lillian faced Jack and whispered, "Tell her right now that you will do whatever she wants; otherwise, you'll die here. She is not a human. She is a demon or something like that." She mouthed a few more words, "Look at her shadow. That's not a human's shadow."

Jack glanced at the ground where Dina's shadow was and saw the jackal-headed figure. He nodded as his eyes locked on his sister's. He understood. If they were to survive, they had to obey this monster. Otherwise, their destiny would be the same as the other archeologists and their workers at the camps.

Jack lifted his head, dark hair falling over his eyes, and addressed Dina. "Yes, I will do whatever you want."

Lillian quickly translated it, and Dina looked pleased.

"You need to help me to find the heart scarab my father wore," Dina repeated. "We don't have much time."

That's good to know, Lillian thought and quickly translated to her brother what Dina had just said.

He asked, "What is this heart scarab? Who was her father? We need to get more facts to find this jewelry."

Lillian asked the questions, and Dina replied, "Thutmose, the high priest of Pharaoh Akhenaten, who became the ruler after the pharaoh died. He was my father. The one who buried me in the tomb. He wore the golden scarab beetle when he was crowned as the regent of the land. He was buried with it when he died, or so I assume."

"That tomb must be where the excavation was done," Lillian said to Jack and explained what else Dina had told her.

Dina waited impatiently. "Slaves. I don't have time to waste. Do you know where my father was buried?"

"I can find out if we know that," Lillian replied, pointing at the tent. "The archeologists who stayed here in this camp have books detailing the archeological findings. I can check if I can find any information about your father and this scarab." Lillian got up, brushed off her pants, and walked to the tent.

Jack climbed out of the sand pit and stayed on the ground. He took deep breaths to calm his racing heart. Then he glanced up and saw Dina staring at him. She said something, but he didn't understand a word. "Lillian is the one who speaks your language," Jack said.

Dina lifted her shoulders and marched to the tent.

Jack's eyes followed her, wondering what kind of a demon she was. She speaks the ancient language, asks to be served as a pharaoh, and looks for a golden scarab... Whatever those archeologists woke and released in that tomb is evil, he concluded. He lingered outside. He hesitated because he didn't want to leave Lillian alone with this demon, but would Dina kill him if he showed any signs of disobedience...

Inside the tent, Lillian picked up the first book on the table and checked the contents for any mention of Dina's father, Thutmose, and Pharaoh Akhenaten. She was an archeologist, but she was not familiar with Thutmose. She had heard of Pharaoh Akhenaten. Though she was unsure which tomb site would be his in the Valley of the Kings, she knew the pharaoh was buried there. She glanced up when Dina walked in and sat next to her.

After reading the chapters dealing with the burial sites, Lillian discovered that many influential priests were buried at a burial site called the Theban Necropolis on the west bank of the river Nile. Thutmose could be there, she thought.

Lillian realized that if the tomb of Thutmose was discovered and raided by either robbers or earlier archeological teams, the golden heart scarab might not be with Dina's father at the tomb anymore.

She had two choices: check out the tombs or check the books in the tent to see if they mentioned the heart scarab and where it was today. She decided it would take them some hours to go to the burial site and check the tombs to see if Thutmose's burial place was even among them. They would have to check each tomb in the area to learn which one was his burial site.

"I know the area where Thutmose was buried. I don't know which tomb there is his. We can go and investigate the tombs," Lillian explained to Dina.

She stood up and said, "We will go now. I don't have much time."

Dina mentioned again that she doesn't have much time. Is there a time restraint on her being out in the world? Why does she need the scarab? Lillian wondered and followed Dina outside where Jack waited for them near the car.

17

The Tombs of Nobles

Jack was the designated driver because Dina wanted to keep Lillian close to her in the backseat and ask her questions about the burial site and the new world. Dina was both frightened and impressed by the new vehicles that did not require horses or camels. It was hard to explain how they worked in the ancient Egyptian language, but Lillian kept trying.

The rolling dunescape all around them looked beautiful but also treacherous. Jack had to keep a steady speed so the car would not roll down a dune, tumble sideways, or sink into quicksand. He mostly followed the route he and her sister had taken to the excavation site and the Brits' camp, but when they got closer to the Nile, he chose to follow the west side of it to reach the burial site of the noblemen and the priests opposite Luxor. Although Lillian could not have been sure that Thutmose had been buried there, this was a place to start. The closer they got to the Nile, the more palm trees and oases were visible. Likewise, some gravel roads appeared when he got closer to the towns and cities built close to the river because of the fishing industry.

The gusty wind picked up, blowing the sand in their eyes. Jack stopped by the roadside and grabbed his driving glasses, pilot's glasses with a headband behind the head, and tied a large white scarf around his head and mouth to avoid inhaling the sand. In the backseat, Lillian did the same with her scarf and took out her large sunglasses.

Dina to the wind, "Away, my darling," and the wind paused, passed the car, and seemed to blow harder all around them. Dina had created an air bubble around the vehicle so they could move to the burial site without delay.

Jack felt the hairs on his neck stand up. *This witch or demon or whatever she is can manipulate the wind too! How do we get rid of her or him? She looks like a man, like our friend Lewis Llewellyn but this creature said her name is Dina and that she is a daughter of Thutmose, a high priest back in Egypt. What did Sir Michael and the German archeologist dig up in that tomb? How could she be alive and talking in Lewis's body if she was supposed to be dead thousands of years ago? Is the real Lewis dead or still inside his body with this creature dominating his actions?*

Jack sighed. He had no answers and couldn't ask Lillian anything because the creature was listening and observing everything.

The wind was making the sand ripple like water, changing the dunes again. *It will be difficult to find the way back to the excavation site again,* Jack thought. Although they had the exact coordinates, the site would probably be buried under the sand.

Half an hour later, Jack pulled off the road again. The road ahead led steeply upwards to where the first tombs were found in the necropolis. "We're here," he announced, glancing back.

The burial site had only partly been excavated, although many archeologists believed there was more to be found. The earthquakes had destroyed many buildings, and archeologists had found partial walls and statues. That was where Lillian believed Dina's father, Thutmose, the high priest of Pharaoh Akhenaten, could be found. She had not seen Thutmose's name in the list of the cataloged and archeologically completed burial temples; thus, she believed it was one of the newer tombs or recent excavations. She had no recent news of what the German archeologists had found in this area, but she hoped her hunch was correct and they would find Dina's father buried here.

"Many noblemen and the priests were buried here," Lillian explained to Dina as they walked uphill.

Jack followed them a few feet behind. The wind had turned into a howling sandstorm creating clouds of sand over the area around them, reducing the visibility almost to zero. However, they still had the protective bubble that Dina had created.

Dina stopped on the next hill and glanced around. She lifted her hands in front of her, palms upwards, and chanted in the ancient language. *A spell of some sort*, Lillian and Jack thought as they watched the sand blow away from the burial site leaving the bare stones and broken walls behind. The different tombs on the site were now visible.

"Is she a demon or a witch or what?" Jack whispered as they watched Dina perform her spell.

"I don't know. Something evil for sure," Lillian replied. "I think she has made a pact with Anubis. Her shadow is part jackal, Anubis's symbol."

"The god of the dead," Jack replied, gritting his teeth. "I should have known. A dead woman comes alive and takes the body of an English man. Of course, the old gods of Egypt have something to do with it."

"I believe her father, the high priest, read a summoning spell and asked a favor from Anubis. Somehow, the god of the dead answered and kept Dina's essence alive to resurrect today. Dina was just his daughter, not an important person, but the father was an influential nobleman. He knew the ways to reach the gods," Lillian whispered back.

Dina turned her black eyes to them and said, "Go down there and look at my father's gravesite."

Lillian quickly walked ahead and started descending to the burial site area. Jack followed her. Dina stayed behind, watching their every move.

"How do we know which one is the right tomb?" Jack asked as they proceeded down the hill.

"We need to find a heart scarab. It's a sort of gold jewelry shaped like a scarab beetle," Lillian said. "If we don't find it, then we haven't found the right burial site."

They walked around the sandstone blocks and partially destroyed and cracked walls of the temples.

"The graverobbers could have found the jewelry and taken it all," Jack commented as they searched the first open temple. It only had one room. The other walls had collapsed, probably during the earthquake. Some of the temples they found had a large granite block under them, so the base was strong enough to withstand the tremors.

"We need tools to get inside the other rooms," Lillian said as she walked into another tomb and found the inside mostly crumbled into a pile of rubble.

So far, they had not found any jewelry in either tomb.

Dina appeared before them and asked if they had located the right tomb.

Lillian replied, "No, your highness. The tombs have collapsed in centuries of sandstorms and earthquakes. We have no idea which one could be your father's tomb."

Dina turned her cold dead eyes to Lillian and replied, "My father would have left a sign outside the tomb for me to find. His sigil included the dunes and the sun with a jackal's head."

She kneeled on the ground and drew the image on the sand with her finger. The dunes were triangular-shaped, the sun was a circle between them, and the jackal head with pointy ears and the stickman body were on the right side of the image. She stood up and wiped the sand off her fingers.

Lillian stared at the image to memorize it, then glanced around the crumbled walls and piles of sandstone. She had not seen that sigil in the previous tombs. "The previous ones didn't have that sigil, although they were badly damaged."

"The sigil would be outside the doorway. My father would have carved it there to help me find his heart scarab," Dina repeated.

Lillian looked at her desperately. *How can we find the tomb that might or might not be here*? she thought. *This site requires months or years of excavation and tools to dig up the gravesite, open the collapsed walls, and find hidden rooms. We don't have any of that.*

"If you don't find the gravesite here, then you and your brother are of no use to me," Dina threatened.

"We will look for it here. The tomb could also be on the other side of the river Nile," Lillian replied calmly. "Besides, you need me to translate your language to ours."

"I don't need your brother." Dina turned her cold eyes to Jack, who shivered. "I'll let him be for now. We might need his muscle strength later," Dina added.

Dina realizes she won't succeed alone either, Lillian thought.

The sun was setting on the horizon, and the air was getting cooler when Lillian and Jack climbed on the last pile of broken sandstones at the burial site. And there, finally, Lillian saw the sigil! "Over here!" she called Dina, who almost flew there.

Lillian and Jack collapsed on the ground, panting. They had checked each of the stones and broken pieces of walls in the area to find that one symbol and had been lucky to find it. They had no idea what Dina would have done to them if they had not succeeded.

Jack offered Lillian a sip of drink from his canister. She took it and swallowed a mouthful. They had to save water because they didn't know if Dina would let them drink or eat anything. She was too focused on finding her father's grave.

Dina kneeled next to the sigil and brushed it with her hand. "It is my father's sigil," she confirmed and looked behind the sandstone where the sigil was placed. Behind it was a temple with an open doorway. She stood up and walked inside.

Lillian and Jack decided it was better to stay where they were. They had already visited inside. It was either robbed or emptied by other archaeologists. They didn't know what Dina would do

Dina emerged, and ordered, "Slaves! Come here."

Ah, we are slaves now, Jack thought and stood up, pulling his sister up. They walked to Dina, and she pointed angrily inside. "The tomb is empty. Someone has taken the sarcophagus and the jewelry with it."

Lillian nodded. "Yes, the tomb is empty."

Dina latched her black eyes on Lillian and said, "I must find the heart scarab. It was here. Where is it now?"

"I can look for the sarcophaguses in my books." Then she remembered all the archeological books were back in the camp. She sighed and added, "We left the books at the camp. We should return there. Now, we know the tomb was here. I can find out where the sarcophagus and the heart scarab have been taken."

Lillian hoped that her explanation was enough to let them live. She had no idea if she could find the sarcophagus anywhere. It was wartime. How would she even do that? She figured if any archeology teams had been out here before or during the war, they must have taken their discoveries to their own countries. The only major players were the Brits and the Germans, so she had two options of where to find the heart stone: London or Berlin.

18

The Mummies

"No!" Dina cried out angrily. She stared at her two prisoners, mumbling something, then took two steps towards the collapsed wall where the sigil was. Her clothes flapped around her in the wind. She stood still with her black eyes wide open.

The sand raised from the ground in the form of a whirling column several feet high, swirling around her in the wind.

"A dust devil!" Jack uttered and pulled Lillian closer to a wall. They pressed against each other and kneeled closer to the stones, hoping they would be safe there. Dina had taken away the safe air bubble, and the wind pulled their clothes and piled sand over them, suffocating them.

"It's because we couldn't find her father's grave here. She's punishing us!" Lillian shouted to her brother, coughing from the sand entering her lungs and nose.

"She asks for the impossible! We can't find a grave in a day when it's been lost for centuries!" Jack replied to her, pressing Lillian's face against her chest.

The wind howled like speaking to the ruins pushing the sand to higher piles. Dina stood still near her father's gravesite amid a sandstorm, seemingly undisturbed. The view of the burial area was obscured by the sand, which was now as thick as a fog. It looked as if she was listening to what the wind and sand told her.

Alas, no. Dina had cast a spell, Lillian realized when she glimpsed at Dina.

The sand belched up mummified bodies, which began to unwrap some of their body wraps to move more freely. Their wraps were musty, dusty, and partly frayed and torn. Soon, Dina had thirty mummies to command.

"Come here!" she barked, and both Jack and Lillian quickly checked to see if the order was for them, but Dina kept her eyes on the mummies and said, "Find Thutmose's heart scarab!"

The mummies started scrambling around, digging up the ground, pushing the stones and broken walls away.

The wind had calmed down. Lillian and Jack brushed the sand from their clothes, and Jack offered her a drink from his canteen, which she gratefully took.

"I think those mummies are the lower priests," Lillian said, keeping her eyes on the mummies. "They are mummified, not buried in the ground like poor people. Besides, they were found in this area, so they must be either noble or priests."

The mummies were extraordinarily efficient and unnaturally strong. They easily lifted the sandstones and parts of walls, unlike any normal living human could. Soon, Thutmose's gravesite was taken apart, the collapsed walls cleared away, and the pathways to the other rooms of the burial chamber were opened. Dina breezed past the mummies to see what was in there. They heard an angry shriek, and she stormed back. "Nothing in any of the rooms!"

Dina raised her chin up and her eyes towards the sky. She wailed to the sky and cast a spell to demolish the mummies and send them back to the ground again. Her furious eyes found Lillian and Jack, and she was about to cast another spell when Jack said, "Let me see if I can find any clues inside where the items might have been taken." He pulled Lillian up and with her to the tomb. *It is safer inside than with Dina anyhow*, Jack thought.

They lit a torch on the wall, and Jack carried it in his hand as they illuminated the rooms.

He saw a cigarette on the corner of the floor. He picked it up and examined it. He showed it to Lillian. "Nazis have been here. The sarcophagus and the jewelry must be in Berlin. They smoke Trommier! It's their favorite brand!"

"Now we know where Dina will want to go next," Lillian said. "How do you think we'll get there in the middle of the war?"

"I have no idea. Perhaps we don't have to go, and she will go alone," Jack suggested.

"She'll kill us. Our only hope to stay alive is if she takes us with her. We need a plane!" Lillian replied and glanced at the doorway, fearing that Dina was coming to look for them.

19

Dina

Dina stood in the sand; her little black beetles surrounded her swarming around like she was the queen of the colony. The mummies hovered closer as if waiting for her orders.

Jack stepped outside, and Dina turned her pitch-black eyes to him. "Wait! We know who has been in the tomb before us. I know where we need to go!"

Dina didn't understand what he said but realized she had to wait for Lillian to translate before killing the siblings. The mummies moved closer to Jack, and he glanced back to see if Lillian was coming out.

And she did. Lillian faced Dina and quickly explained what Jack had said. The scent of musty fabric filled her nose as the mummies gathered around her.

Jack held out his hand and showed the cigarette butt. "This is the proof. I know I'm right." Dina's chilling gaze was on him. She marched to him and viewed the butt in his hand.

"I don't know what that is."

Jack felt his throat closing. Dina made a quick move in the air with her hand, squeezing the air from him. He coughed, and his face turned red.

"Stop! Please," Lillian pleaded, her eyes wide with terror. She hated seeing her brother suffering like this.

"It's hard to explain because, in your time, you didn't have cigarettes," Lillian started. "Some people smoke them for fun. This one is from Germany. That's where we believe your father's jewelry and sarcophagus are now."

Dina released her grip.

"Thank you," Jack whispered, speaking over his strangled breaths.

"Let's go then," Dina ordered and marched toward the jeep.

"Um, there is a small problem," Lillian said as she tried to keep up with Dina.

Dina gave her an icy look and stopped raising her hand again, aiming her fingers at Jack.

"No! Stop, please," Lillian begged. "We'll come with you, but we can't go to Germany in a car. We need to cross the Mediterranean Sea and then travel through several countries. It will take us days to go by sea and land."

Dina's eyes never left Lillian's face as tears pricked her eyes. Dina lowered her hand and answered with a haughty voice, "That's not acceptable. I don't have that much time. I need to find the scarab in less than seventy-two hours."

Dina slipped with the exact number of hours she had left on earth, Lillian thought. *Good! Now, we know she is fallible. Anubis must have set a time limit. Something will happen to her if she does not find the scarab in seventy-two hours.*

Swallowing hard, Jack approached Lillian and Dina, wondering the best way to handle this monster controlling them. He nodded to Lillian and said, "We need to get a plane or Zeppelin." Lillian tried to explain in ancient language what Jack said, but she had difficulty explaining that they would have to fly to the destination. Finally, she believed Dina had understood.

"Let's move. We need to find that flying vehicle and go to Germany," Dina ordered.

"It's not that easy," Jack started but closed his mouth quickly when Dina glared at him.

"Let's go to Cairo and see if we can find a plane or Zeppelin to rent," Lillian said, grabbing Jack by his hand and pulling him to the Jeep. "We can't argue with her. She's too powerful. She might be able to get us the plane with her powers."

"I can fly a plane, but I can't fly Zeppelin," Jack said. "The problem is that we are going to Germany, and we are Brits. They are our enemies. How do you think we will survive that trip?"

Lillian sat in the passenger seat, and Dina took the back seat. Jack was again the driver.

Lillian sighed. "I don't know. We have to try. She won't give us a chance to get away alive until she has that scarab in her hands."

The mummies stood still and waited for Dina to command them. Dina waved her hand in the air, and the mummies rushed after them, leaping over the dunes and following the car's tracks in the sand.

20

Hotel Alhambra

A few palm trees were swaying in the wind when we approached Cairo. The city was busy with cafes, hotels, and bars filled with foreign visitors from all over the world, even when the war was going on. The locals were dressed in ankle-length caftans, turbans, skull caps, or fezzes.

Dina ordered the mummies to follow them discreetly, so they climbed on the side of the buildings, ran across the roofs, and jumped over the narrow passageways between the houses following the car.

Jack drove along the stone-covered narrow streets surrounded by white buildings through stone archways leading to even narrower and darker alleys, heading to the hotel Alhambra. He hoped to find a pilot there. He didn't care if it was a Brit or a German. He needed one badly because otherwise, he would most likely be killed by the monster in the backseat.

He parked in front of the hotel's entrance and asked Lillian to tell Dina that he would go inside and find out if any pilots were available. Dina was already staring at Lillian with those fathomless eyes that didn't belong to any living person. Jack jumped out of the car, walked past the small outside tables with some guests enjoying their day, and went inside. He was sure if there were any pilots, they would be here having a drink. Where else would they be?

Inside, the hotel's lobby had a minty smell in the air. The lobby had some wicker chairs with small tables, and Jack noted a couple of Englishmen sitting by the tables reading the newspapers. The news was a few weeks old, but most likely the latest they had received. As Jack walked through the lobby heading to the bar, the fans rotated slowly on the ceiling. The bartender was washing glasses when he sat down by the counter. Jack greeted him, ordered a whisky, and paid for it with cash.

The bartender was a carrot top with deep lines on his cheeks and forehead telling his age. He had a potbelly covered by a white shirt and black pants.

Our archeological trip in Egypt has gotten off to a shitty start, Jack thought as he ordered another drink, pulled out a few notes from his pocket, and threw them on the counter. He drank the second drink slowly and then asked the bartender, "Do you know if there are any pilots here?"

The bartender wiped the counter while answering, "Yes, there are two. One is German. The other is a fortune hunter and smuggler who will do anything for the right price."

"Where can I find them?" Jack asked.

'The German is sitting over there with his countrymen. I don't think you want to interrupt him right now. They are celebrating Germany's *blitz attack* on the Soviet Union, believing they will be in Leningrad by September. They plan to win the war this autumn, or so I've heard," the bartender replied and nodded to the group dressed in Germany's military uniforms in a booth and drinking heavily.

Jack nodded and asked, "Where's the other one?"

"He's that one," the bartender replied, pointing at the man resting on the counter and snoring loudly. His shirt was dirty white, his khaki pants brown, and he had long, knee-high brown boots. His wide-brimmed hat was on the chair next to him, and he had a pistol on a holster in his belt.

"Is he drunk?" Jack asked and got up from his chair and walked to the pilot.

"He drinks whenever he gets paid, and he had money last night and used it on drinks. Several drinks, if I may say so," the bartender added. "I couldn't get him to move, so I left him sleeping there. I'd be grateful if you woke him and took him with you. He'll have a hangover when he wakes up, and he's not friendly when he's out of money and drinks."

Of course, he's a drunken pilot, Jack thought. *What else could go wrong on this trip?*

The bartender leaned toward Jack and said, "He is also the best pilot in Cairo. He knows the best ways to smuggle items in and out, even if it's war. If you have a dodgy proposition, then he's your man. Meet Captain Roy Sawyer."

He went to the sleeping man, tapped him lightly on the shoulder, and stepped back quickly to avoid his aim. The man pulled out his gun faster than Jack had ever seen anyone do and pointed it around him, swaying a bit.

"Who was it?" Sawyer asked, looking around. A strand of his brown hair was hanging on his forehead, while the rest of his hair was greased to keep it in style.

"It was just me, Sawyer," the bartender said calmly.

"Oh, okay. Can I have another drink?" Sawyer asked, sitting back on his chair.

"I'll pay for it," Jack replied and gestured to the bartender to give Sawyer a drink.

"Who are you?" Sawyer asked, his eyes still wild-looking.

"I've got a proposition for you. I need a pilot," Jack replied and moved to sit next to Sawyer.

"Where do you want to go?" Sawyer asked.

"To Berlin," Jack replied quietly, glancing at the booth where the Germans were celebrating their war news.

Sawyer coughed as he had drunk into the wrong pipe and wiped his mouth with his sleeve. "Are you nuts! No one wants to go there. There's a war in Europe!"

"I have no choice. See, I have two women with me who need to go there," Jack replied.

"That's worse. Women are bad luck in planes," Sawyer said and gestured for one more drink.

"The other one is not exactly a woman. She looks like a man, but she's more of a monster. Her name is Dina, and she's the daughter of an ancient high priest of Egypt," Jack explained.

"What have you been drinking? I'd like to have the same," Sawyer said, shaking his head in disbelief.

"You can meet my sister and the monster. They are waiting for us outside in a car. They are probably getting impatient as I didn't think this would take this long," Jack replied and glanced at the doorway, making sure Dina wasn't walking in with her mummies.

"We also have a group of mummies following us," he added, shrugging.

Sawyer laughed aloud, alerting the Germans, who looked at them but soon returned to their celebratory drinking. "You're crazy!" Sawyer said and stared at Jack.

Jack shook his head. "No, I'm not. I wouldn't believe me either, but it's true."

"How much would I get paid?" Sawyer asked.

"I don't know. That's up to our daughter of darkness, Dina," Jack replied. "Do you want to meet her?"

"Yes, of course," Sawyer said, not believing a word what Jack had told him. He got up and grabbed his hat. "Right outside, you said?" he asked.

"Yes, my car is parked outside," Jack confirmed and followed Sawyer.

Lillian looked scared at first, but when her eyes met Jack, she seemed relieved. Dina looked impatient.

Jack and Sawyer went to the car, and Jack asked, "Lillian, can you ask Dina what she will pay our pilot if he takes us to Berlin?"

Lillian quickly translated as best as she could. Dina answered, "I'll spare his life."

Lillian turned to Sawyer and said, "She said you can keep your life."

Sawyer laughed. "Funny man!" Dina still looked like Lewis Llewellyn, the archeologist, and not like the woman she was.

Dina held out her hand and wriggled her fingers. A coral snake slithered from her arm and jumped onto Sawyer's shoulder. The snake opened his mouth, showing its venomous teeth, ready to bite him on the neck. Dina asked, "Will you take us to Berlin or not? This snake will kill you instantly."

Lillian translated again.

Sawyer swallowed and sweat shined on his forehead. "Yes, I will. Get this snake of yours off me."

Dina gestured towards the snake, and it disappeared into thin air.

Sawyer frowned. "Was that a magic trick? Where did the snake go?"

Lillian replied, "No, it wasn't a trick. She's a demon or something like that, and she can kill us all easily. She has about 65 hours left. I don't know what will happen after that, but I know she needs to get to Berlin and find her father's sarcophagus and a heart stone buried with him."

Sawyer looked at Lillian as if she were as crazy as her brother. "You both talk like that man in the backseat is a woman. Dina, you called her."

Lillian said, "Yes, that's her name. Dina, the daughter of Thutmose, the high priest of Egypt who reigned there around 1300 BC."

"Are you telling me this man, or a woman, is thousands of years old?" Sawyer said, pushing his hat on the back of his head.

"Yes, that's correct. She is. She killed all the archeologists in both German and British camps and their local helpers. She left us alive because she needed a translator, that's me, and Jack because he could drive the car. Please, believe me, and don't cross her. You'll get yourself killed. The easiest way to please her is to take her to Berlin and find that sarcophagus with the stone." Lillian looked more sad than terrified. She'd seen what Dina could do, but Sawyer had not.

"Okay. My plane is on the outskirts of Cairo. We can get there in fifteen minutes," Sawyer said and jumped in on the car's passenger side. Jack drove.

21

Jack and Sawyer

The sun was setting, coloring the sky with a reddish and orange hue. The earlier sandstorm had disappeared, and the wind had calmed down.

Jack drove through the maze of dark and narrow streets toward the airport where Sawyer said his plane was. Jack had been to Cairo a couple of times before, so he knew the main streets and how to get through the city.

"How did you find this monster sitting behind me?" Sawyer whispered almost without moving his lips.

"Dina does not understand what we say. She speaks an ancient Egyptian language from thousands of years ago. Lillian is the only one who can translate that," Jack replied with a normal voice. "And to answer your question: We went to join the British excavation near the Valley of the Kings only to find out that they were all dead. So were the German archeologists. This monster, as you referred to her, saw us arrive at the camp. We didn't suspect anything. She looked like Lewis Llewellyn, the assistant archeologist. Soon we found out she was something else, a demon perhaps."

"Good, because after I take you to Berlin, I will kill you," Sawyer swore.

"Unless the monster kills us all first," Jack replied somberly. He glanced at Sawyer and added, "It's more likely that none of us will survive this trip regardless of the ongoing war. The danger is not where we are going but in the back seat of this car."

"Yes, I see what you mean," Sawyer replied. "What else can she do but magically create deadly snakes in front of you?"

Jack sighed. "She can bury you in a quicksand, throttle you with mummy wraps, or just with nothing at all. She can kill you with a simple move of her hand. She also has a huge colony of scarab beetles that obey her every command. You have not met those yet. They can eat you alive in minutes or even seconds."

Sawyer shivered as he suddenly felt cold. "We'll see what happens in Berlin," he grunted his reply and kept his eyes on the street ahead.

Jack grinned. He was sure he had won Sawyer to his side. *The enemy of your enemy is your friend*, Jack thought. Dina was their enemy; thus, Jack should join their efforts to conquer her and send her back to where she came from.

The shadows were darker and crept closer to the car as Jack drove through the narrow alleys, and the few lights they saw came from the candles or lights inside the houses. The full moon was higher up in the indigo-blue sky when they finally reached the small side airport with a couple of hangars. The airport was a too fancy name for it. It was more like a tiny airstrip with rundown sheds pretending to be airplane hangars.

Jack was glad that Sawyer's plane was not in the main airport because he didn't want to deal with either Nazis or the Egyptian authorities when they left the country.

Earlier in 1940, Italy's troops had invaded Egypt. The Italian military had taken over the main airport to get their troops and weapons to the continent of Africa and to block access to the airport.

Also, Adolf Hitler had planned to launch Operation *Sonnenblume* at the beginning of 1941 to capture more lands with his General Rommel and the *Afrikakorps*. The Nazis planned to occupy Libya and Tunisia and move forcefully from west to east Africa, pushing the Brits away from the continent. Both the Nazis and the Brits were preparing for a battle they knew was imminent. However, in 1940, the city still accepted visitors from any country to its hotels and bars.

22

The New Plan

"Park over there, next to that second building," Sawyer instructed and pointed to the shacks at the other end of the runaway. There was no light except the moon in the sky at the airstrip.

After Jack had turned off the engine, Sawyer jumped out and pushed the heavy door open, revealing his airplane inside the hangar. He turned on the light by pulling a string that barely lit the hangar and said, "Here is my baby."

He had a Ford trimotor in the hangar. The plane was partially covered with a cotton tarp.

"Is that plane in working condition?" Jack asked, raising his eyebrows. It was an older plane than what he had expected to see.

"Yes, of course. This *Tin Goose has* been serving faithfully since I won it in a poker game in Paris." Sawyer patted the side of the plane affectionally and then pulled off the rest of the tarp to the ground.

"Now we need to get some gas if we plan to fly to Berlin without any extra stops," Sawyer said. "We can fly about 500 miles per day, and Berlin is about 1800 miles away."

Jack shook his head. "No, that won't do. We need to get to Berlin in two days. Dina has less than three days left to find the scarab she's looking for. I think the time is closer to sixty hours now."

"In that case, we'd need a DC-2 or DC-3 because they would need one stop, and we'd be in Berlin in two days," Sawyer commented. He looked pensive, then added, "Or a Zeppelin would take us there in nine to ten hours."

"Where can we get one of those? Because if we don't get Dina to Berlin in less than 2 days, she will kill us here. She will not need us," Jack warned Sawyer.

"I know. She already demonstrated how easily she can kill," Sawyer replied. "If you want to go with Germans in a Zeppelin, I know where it is now. The only problem is that the Germans will check the tickets on board and throw you out if you don't have a valid ticket."

"We don't have tickets." Jack pushed his hands into the front pockets of his pants and frowned. "Can you fly one?" Jack asked.

"I think so. I would assume it can't be more difficult than flying an airplane, although I have never flown one before," Sawyer said. "If you plan to capture a Zeppelin, then I have to warn you: Nazis are watching over the aircraft with hawk eyes, and the soldiers will capture anyone who is not authorized to be near or inside it."

"We'll have one advantage," Jack replied. He nodded outside to the car and said, "Dina."

"You're right. She can kill anyone who goes against her, and they can't kill her. How do we get her to go with our plan?" Sawyer asked.

"Let's talk to Lillian, and she can explain to Dina that we need to steal a Zeppelin from Nazis. I'm not sure if she will understand any of that, but she will understand that a Zeppelin is much faster than the small aircraft you have here."

They walked together outside and presented the plan to Lillian, who translated it to Dina. Lillian agreed with the men that it was the only way they would reach Berlin in less than three days.

"The faster we reach our destination, the better," Dina replied. "My mummies will help take over the plane."

23

The Zeppelin

After Hindenburg and her sister ship, the LZ 130 Graf Zeppelin II were built, and the disaster with Hindenburg happened in 1937, several blimps were still made for air travel. The current one was ready to leave as soon as the passengers were boarded. The Nazi soldiers in their grey uniforms guarded the airship. Some high-level officers of SS and *Afrikakorps* had planned to travel to Berlin, thus the extra security on the airstrip.

Jack parked further away by the terminal and surveyed the area.

"They must be waiting for someone important because it's already night, and they are still here. I was sure they would have gone earlier and then returned tomorrow morning. I guess we're lucky," Sawyer said. "Although, now we are more at risk of being shot than on any other day."

The Nazi soldiers stood guard by the steps leading up to the blimp. The steward stood on top of the stairs, looking nervous. He knew they were late. The food would be cold in the dining room, and the guests would be angry and complain, but he could do nothing about it. If a field marshal were coming onboard, they'd have to stay here and wait for him. Also, he wouldn't instruct the pilots to leave without the SS officers. The steward knew there would be more trouble if they did so than stayed and waited for them. He glanced back when he heard some passengers already complaining about being late and shrugged. He stepped back inside to calm them.

Outside the terminal, Jack considered their plan and how to get on board. They had no tickets. They would be stopped by the door. The only way in was with Dina. Dina had to take down the soldiers, then they could climb onboard. If the pilots and passengers didn't fight back, they would have a smooth flight to Berlin.

"Lillian, can you ask Dina to deal with those soldiers next to the aircraft?" Jack said and got up from the driver's seat.

Lillian spoke with Dina, who stared at her and then nodded. She opened the backdoor and climbed out, lifting her hand and calling out her mummies. They appeared from the shadows and stood hovering next to her. She told them in ancient language to attack the men on the ground.

They all turned to see what the mummies would do. Lillian and Jack had a pretty good idea, but Sawyer had not seen the mummies at work. The mummies appeared silently from behind and on each side and pounced on the unwary soldiers biting their necks like vampires and cutting their heads off. A messy incident, but fast, Jack thought. The mummies stood still by the aircraft waiting for more orders.

"Let's go!" Jack said, and their little group headed to the Zeppelin.

Jack knew they didn't have much time, so better go now, when the soldiers were down.

At first, when the steward returned to the doorway, he didn't notice anything was off. However, when his eyes adjusted to the darkness, he saw some movement on the side of the aircraft in the shadows. He tried to see who, hoping they were the missing passengers, but these figures were too skinny, and their appearance wasn't soldierlike.

"What's going on?" the steward murmured, stepping a few steps down the stairs and trying to see better into the shadows.

"Good evening," Jack called out in German and waved his hand at the steward. He walked to the airship and told Sawyer, "Remove the ropes that keep the Zeppelin on the ground. We'll have to go fast before more Nazis arrive." Sawyer ran under the airship and started opening each rope that held it on the ground, and then when he'd done his job, he walked up the stairs.

The steward, a lean and tall man in his forties, wore a white jacket a white shirt under it, and dark blue pants. He saw a group approaching Zeppelin:

two men and two women. *Perhaps these are the guests we are waiting for,* he thought happily.

When the group climbed the stairs, the steward noticed their outfits were civilian, not SS or Nazi uniforms. He stayed by the doorway and waited for the group to come to the doorway light. The men who had called out on him said, “Lovely night for a flight.”

The steward realized he spoke in English. “What is this? Do you have tickets?”

Jack glanced at Dina, who gestured with her fingers, and the steward felt a sharp pain in his chest like someone had grabbed his heart and squeezed it hard. He fell on the floor, gasping, but he was not dead yet. By then, Sawyer had caught up with them.

“Ah, good,” Jack said, glancing inside. The dining room, with the white tablecloths and red upholstered metal chairs, looked ready for a late dinner. “I was getting hungry.”

Jack nodded to Sawyer, who gave a thumbs-up in response. 'Take Dina and Lillian to the cockpit and brief the pilots,' Jack instructed. He then turned to the steward, who was seated by the doorway, and offered, "Let me close that for you." Jack stepped over the steward's outstretched legs, pulled the door shut, and warned, "We're ready for departure. If you value your life, I suggest you board quickly." With that, Jack headed towards the dining room, leaving the steward to scramble into action.

Sawyer nodded and took the ladies to the front of the blimp. He knocked on the door, and when the pilot opened the door, Sawyer said, “Good evening. We need to borrow your aircraft. We are going to Berlin, but if you don't want to fly us there, then I will do it."

The pilot in his dark blue uniform frowned and said, "Is this a joke?"

His co-pilot, a young man in his twenties, turned to follow the conversation by the door.

"No, I'm afraid not. We have an urgent business in Berlin," Lillian said, smiling apologetically.

"Miss, if you're a passenger, then take your seat. Otherwise, get out of the aircraft, or I will call the soldiers to arrest you and take you to the nearest SS interrogation," the pilot warned, turning red in the face with anger.

Sawyer saw that the talk would not help them, so he said, "Dina, would you please help this pilot to understand?" Lillian translated it for Dina.

Dina lifted her arms, and a colony of beetles appeared out of nowhere and attacked the pilot. He was a pile of bones in seconds.

Sawyer stepped over the bones and said, "That's taken care of. Now, we need to leave before more Nazis arrive." He glanced at the copilot and asked, "Are you with us or against us?"

The co-pilot stared at the bones on the floor and swallowed. "With you. Where do you want to go?"

"Berlin," Sawyer said. He turned his head and said, "Lillian, take the monster to the passenger area and have a seat. We're taking off in minutes."

He turned to the copilot and said, "Let's do this."

The co-pilot nodded.

The Zeppelin turned the helium vents on to make the aircraft buoyant in the surrounding air, so the Zeppelin rose upwards in the air. The copilot quickly throttled the engine and adjusted the elevators to angle the airship into the wind coming from the south.

Sawyer surveyed the airport and noticed two army jeeps approaching the terminal. *Too late*, he thought. *Those must have been the late-arriving guests.* The vehicles parked where Zepp had been a few minutes ago and stared upwards. Sawyer could see the angry gestures of the passengers in the vehicles.

Jack had taken a table with a window view in the dining room and saw the army vehicles too. He sipped his drink, which he had served himself, then glanced around. Many paying passengers looked rich and had lots of jewels on them. This was a fine dining restaurant, a luxury trip. His clothes didn't match theirs, and thus, he got frowning looks.

Lillian and Dina joined him.

"Everything okay?" he asked. Lillian nodded. "Yes, the co-pilot and Sawyer are flying this blimp. The pilot is dead."

"Ah, great. I hope the flight is smooth and we'll be in Berlin in no time. While Sawyer is flying, I think we should enjoy the dinner here," Jack said to Lillian. "I'm hungry."

24

Inside the Blimp

"What happened to the mummies?" Jack asked Lillian.

"I'm not sure. I think they might be onboard," Lillian replied.

"They didn't come inside after us. I closed the door," Jack insisted.

"They might be on top of this airship or hang outside. They are somewhere. Dina wanted them to travel with us," Lillian replied.

Then they heard a shrill scream. “Outside! There’s a skeleton or a mummy!”

An elderly woman pointed outside, and there was one of the mummies hanging behind the window. Jack leaned closer and saw the other mummies hanging from the lines on the side of the blimp. “Ah, mystery solved.” He poured some more wine into his glass, ignoring the dining room commotion.

Down below, the bright spotlights were directed upwards to the night sky. The Nazis gathered below the blimp, looking upwards, their eyes following Zepp as it gained distance.

“No shooting! This Zeppelin could explode like Hindenburg!” the Field Marshal instructed. “We can’t lose it.” He grabbed the binoculars. “What are those things hanging on the ropes on the surface?” he asked and handed the binoculars to his assistant, who took them. “They look like mummies! They are all wrapped in layers of cloth from head to toe.”

“That’s impossible! Why would the airship have mummies hanging on the sides?” the Field Marshal commented. “They must be spies disguised as mummies. They will freeze up there or get tired of hanging there and fall to imminent death.” He faced his assistant and said, “It’s time to call Berlin and our headquarters. The spies can’t reach the city.”

“We don’t know where they are heading. We don’t even know if the spies took over the aircraft. The pilot might have spotted them and lifted off before they got inside,” the assistant replied and turned his face to the sky again. “He might have saved the aircraft from getting into the hands of the enemy.”

"Let's try to contact the pilot and find out," the Field Marshal replied and marched back to his car and ordered the messenger, "Call the zeppelin and find out what happened. Why didn't they wait for us like they were ordered?"

Inside the blimp, the passengers who sat by the windows looked down and asked questions in German: "What's going on?" "Why are they lighting the sky?" "It's the army!"

They were dressed for a fine dining event with fancy clothes and expensive jewelry, and the crew supplied them with newspapers and magazines to read during the flight. Most of the passengers were either officers or their wives. Men wore military uniforms: SS officer had their feared black uniforms, *Heer* grey uniforms, olive green *Afrikakorps*, *Kriegsmarine* midnight blue, and *Luftwaffe* blue-grey dress uniforms. A few key industrialists were onboard as well: Carl Bosch, who was the founder of I.G. Farben chemical factories, Alfried Krupp of Krupp Group, who manufactured weapons for the Nazis, and Friedrich Flick of Flick companies, who was instrumental in providing ammunition, coal, and steel works for Germany.

"Achtung! Achtung! Pilots on board the blimp. Land immediately!" the message echoed inside the cockpit. Sawyer and the copilot ignored it. The co-pilot received another message from Cairo airport telling him to land immediately. He faced Sawyer and said, "The army is asking me to land immediately."

"Keep flying. I'll go and find our resident mummy. She'll take care of them," Sawyer said and left the cockpit. He found Dina with Jack and

Lillian in the dining room. "We need some help. The Nazis are asking us to land."

The officers onboard heard his comment. "What is going on?" One of the Luftwaffe's officers came to stand next to their table. "Is there something wrong with the pilots? Because if there is, I'm capable of flying this aircraft too."

"No, nothing is wrong," Sawyer replied.

"You're not German. How did you get on board?" The SS officer looked sternly at Sawyer. Then his gaze went over the group on the table, all looking ragged and dusty, and he added, "I don't think you have tickets. Show me your passports."

Jack glanced at him and took another sip of his wine. "Sorry, I don't think we have any passports with us. You need to talk to our trip coordinator." He nodded to Dina, who turned her bottomless black eyes to the two officers standing next to their table. Lillian explained what was wrong.

Dina leaned back on his chair. She lifted her hand, and the mummy wraps appeared from thin air, wrapped around the officers' necks, and started strangling. The men fell to the floor. While the two officers were gasping on the floor, the other German officers turned their focus to Dina.

"What is this? Are you a magician?" one of them asked stepping closer to the dying officers. "Let them go!" he tried to untie the wraps around their necks, but it was no use. It was as if they were glued to their skin. The men kicked their legs on the floor, tried to get their fingers under the wraps to loosen them, struggled for a while, and then gave up and died.

"I'm sorry. I don't think Dina cares if they die or not. If I were you, I would leave her alone," Jack replied. His voice was indifferent. He knew that Dina could kill them all if she wished to.

The officers glanced at Dina, who stared at them with her emotionless eyes and backed away. She looked like a young Englishman but emitted the power of ancient evil with her gaze. Her eyes were not human.

"Dina, can you do something about the groups at the airport we left from?" Sawyer asked. Lillian translated again.

Dina stepped to the window and glanced up. She gestured to the mummies hanging on the side of the blimp. Two of them jumped down, creating havoc on the ground pulling hearts out, cutting heads off, and ripping limbs off bodies. No soldiers or officers were left alive after they were done. The mummies could not climb back on the aircraft, so they stayed behind. Dina gestured, and their bodies disintegrated to dust.

Jack sighed and said to Sawyer, "Okay, Dina solved your little problem. You can go back to the cockpit. I don't think anyone will bother you for a while unless the Nazis decide to bomb this airship down."

Sawyer brushed his hair back with his hand. "Should I feel sorry that a few more Nazis are dead because of me?"

Jack shook his head. "No, it's not because of you. It's all about Dina and her wishes. We are all here because of her. We're only alive because that's what she wants now."

Sawyer returned to the cockpit. He was not sure what he had gotten into, but he was not sure if he or any of the others inside this aircraft would survive this flight. The mummies swayed outside, hanging on the ropes on the side of the blimp. The aircraft looked like a vessel of death in the moonlight than a normal passenger blimp.

Inside, the passengers settled down and took their seats by the windows or dining room. The tables next to Dina were left empty. The flight attendants started to serve the dinner and drinks as if this was a normal flight.

25

The Flight

The night sky was dark and speckled with stars. No clouds. The Zeppelin flew quietly with a speed of 78 miles per hour towards the north and Berlin.

Sawyer glanced at the co-pilot. "You can go and have dinner if you like. I got this."

"Okay, I don't mind if I do," the copilot replied, adding, "My name is Niels. Niels Kruger." He extended his hand to Sawyer, who gave him a surprised look.

"Nice to meet you." Sawyer shook his hand. "I'm not in control of what that monster does, you know. I'm obeying orders like anyone else."

"I realized that. What is she? You talk like she is a woman, and her name is female: Dina, but he looks like a man," Niels asked.

"I'm not the expert on this topic. You should ask Lillian and Jack. They pulled me into this horror. As far as I know, she is a mummy risen from death. She took the body of a young archeologist. Lillian and Jack met her at the excavation camp near the tomb, where she was released to this world to cause terror and reign. In her previous life, she was a woman. She didn't have much choice in what or whose body she possessed. She had to pick the one that came to the tomb. That's only my guess. Lillian might know more," Sawyer replied, staring outside. The Zeppelin flew steadily, and there was not much to do.

"Okay, thanks," Niels replied. "I'll be back soon, and I can fly then while you eat."

"Sure. We can take turns in breaks, too," Sawyer said. He turned his head to face the co-pilot. "Please, be careful out there. Dina is a monster, a mummy alive. She is not human. Don't aggravate her. I don't want to land this aircraft by myself, and I plan to live a few more years if she doesn't kill us right now."

Nils nodded and left the cockpit. He headed to the dining room. He noticed the small group sitting separately from the other passengers and sat at one of the empty tables. Nils ordered a chicken dinner from the flight attendant, and after he left, Nils looked around. He saw that the Nazi officers were sitting now at one table planning something.

Hopefully, they won't try to take over the cockpit or attack Dina, Nils thought as he glanced at the German military officials. He swallowed his doubts as he was sure the officers would not let the capture of their prize zeppelin go without any resistance. His only hope was that they would not cause the death of all onboard.

After Nils had gotten his drink, and a glass of soda water, Jack moved his chair closer to Nils and asked, "How is it going in the cockpit?"

"Good, Sawyer is now flying this aircraft," Nils replied. He whispered, "What are you going to do if the officers plan to attack you?"

Jack shrugged. "Nothing. Dina will do her tricks."

"Is she that powerful?" Nils asked. He had not seen what Dina had done to the two officers on board nor what had happened at the airport below the aircraft.

"She is the most powerful creature I've ever met," Jack confirmed.

Dina turned her black eyes to them and asked, "What are you two talking about?" Lillian, of course, translated immediately, as that was her job.

Jack nodded toward the officers' table and said, "We wondered if the officers realize who you are and what you can do. They seem to be planning something." He had decided to play on Dina's team for now. He knew that if he sided with the Nazis, he would lose because they would imprison him and torture him. He was not a German but a Brit and, thus, their enemy.

Slowly, Dina turned her head to the table where the officers sat whispering together.

She lifted her hands, and the black beetles scurried down her arms and legs. They ran to the officers and attacked. In seconds, the officers started screaming and brushing away the crawling flesh-eating bugs. The other passengers vomited, cried in horror, and passed out when they saw the carnage. The beetles returned to Dina within minutes, leaving the skeletons in uniforms behind.

"This can't be real. Perhaps the helium gas is leaking, and we are all hallucinating," one of the industrial tycoons said. All the remaining passengers were unsure if they were living a nightmare or hallucinating –except Lillian, Jack, and Sawyer, who already knew what Dina was capable of and had witnessed it before.

Jack sighed and poured more wine into his and Lillian's glasses. "Let's drink some more." He offered some to Nils, who had a greenish tint to his face. "You should have something to drink," Jack suggested as he saw Nils swallow hard a few times, then lean down and vomit next to the table. "You'll get used to the killing after a while," Jack commented to Nils, lifting the glass and emptying it.

Dina sat still. Her eyes surveyed the passengers but didn't stop on anyone in particular. She was more curious about the women aboard and their dresses. She asked Lillian to explain the clothing. "The women here wear the latest style," Lillian started. "The silhouette is slim with broad, squared shoulders. The fabric is cotton or wool. The skirts billow around the calves or end just below the knee. Blouses have padded shoulders like that woman over there," Lillian pointed at one of the ladies sitting by the window. Dina stared at the woman and said, "If she wasn't that old, I would take her body. I don't like being a man."

Lillian cringed inside.

Dina's eyes scanned the passengers and paused on a young woman in her twenties. She assessed the young woman from top to toe and said with an affirmative tone, "She would do."

Lillian frowned. *What is Dina planning now?*

Dina stood up, walked to the woman with lazy steps, and stopped next to her seat. The young woman had dark brown hair just below her shoulders. She was slim, with a narrow waist, and her face was oval with dark brown eyes. The woman glanced at Dina curiously.

"You'll give me a new body," Dina commanded. She had waited for a suitable body since she met Lillian. She didn't take Lillian's because she was more valuable as a translator.

The young woman didn't understand Dina and frowned. A slight touch of an invisible hand caressed her face and hair, and a thin stream of smoke exited from Lewis's body, entering the young woman's nose and mouth. Lewis's body crumbled, dead. It was only flesh and bones now with no soul inside. The chosen woman grabbed her throat and looked around the aircraft in a panic. Her eyes changed from brown to black, and her body spasmed, then went limp in the chair.

"Mine!" Dina's voice came from inside the young woman's body.

Dina inhaled deeply and sat up, glancing at her new body, lifting her arms and wiggling her fingers. "It is great to have a woman's body again,"

Dina said, looking pleased, returning to the dining room. Horrified stares followed Dina's every move. Casually, Dina sat down at the table and viewed the dining room.

26

At Himmler's Office

Even though it was the middle of the night, SS-Reichsführer Heinrich Himmler was fully dressed and stood in front of a large world map. His assistant, Werner Grothman, greeted the officer formally with his right hand and arm straight in front of him, "Sieg Heil!"

Himmler turned and asked, "Any news?"

Werner Grothman replied, "No word from Egypt. The tomb was scheduled to be entered early yesterday morning. Now, it's past midnight, and no word from the archeologists."

Himmler frowned, walked to his desk, and sat down on the leather chair. "You have tried to contact the camp, but no one answers. That would mean that there's no one to answer the calls. I suggest we send someone from Afrikakorps to search the campsite and the tomb and find out what happened. The soldiers are close by, and it would only take them about an hour to get to that site." Himmler gestured with his hand for Werner to leave the room.

Werner saluted him and left the room. He stepped behind his desk and called the army's headquarters in North Africa. After the call, he sat down and waited for the next contact. He feared that the news they would receive would not be good.

Werner rubbed his face with his hands to keep him awake. He had been up since the sunrise of the previous morning, keeping up with Himmler's speed. Himmler needed only two-three to hours of sleep and expected anyone at his office to be awake when he was. Extra hours of sleep were a luxury, which didn't happen often. Werner closed his eyes. He could take a cat nap here, and no one would notice. He would hear if a call came from Africa or Himmler needed him. He put his head on top of his arms on the desktop and closed his eyes.

Two hours later, a phone rang.

Werner was startled from a deep sleep. He quickly grabbed the phone's handset and answered. After the formal greetings, Werner's face grew somber. “Repeat that, please.” He had to confirm he had heard the other party correctly. It could not be true! He ended the call and rushed to knock on Himmler’s door. He almost ran in without waiting for his superior officer to reply but then calmed himself down. *No, I must wait*, he told himself. *SS-Reichsführer might be in the middle of some strategic planning with Berlin. I can’t interrupt him.*

Werner had to wait a couple more minutes before Himmler asked him to enter. “News from Africa?” SS-Reichsführer Heinrich Himmler asked immediately. His hazel-colored eyes were sharp as he faced Werner.

“Yes, SS-Reichsführer,” Werner replied.

“Tell me.” Himmler leaned back in his chair, his eyes never leaving his assistant’s face.

“They are all dead,” Werner blurted out without thinking. The news of the excavation site was so strange that he had not thought about how to present it to his superior officer.

“Explain!” Himmler ordered and slammed his hand on the desktop.

“The tomb was opened and empty. Both the German archeologists were dead. Their bodies were identified by their clothing, as no flesh remained on their bones. Notably, one of the British archaeologists was also found in a skeletal state, a grim reminder of the devastating fate that befell the group. All the excavation workers had been killed the same way, and both camps were empty. I mean empty. No one was alive. No Germans, no Brits, and no local workers.”

“Ach!” Himmler said, forming a steeple with his hands in front of him. “Anything else?”

"Maybe. There was a note that two Brits were arriving yesterday. A brother and a sister: Jack and Lillian Stiller. Lillian Stiller is a young archeologist. Also, one British archeologist called Lewis Llewellyn is missing. The soldiers could not find any trails leaving or coming to the camps because of a sandstorm yesterday. They contacted Cairo and found out that the Stillers left their hotel to go to the British camp yesterday." Werner stopped there. He didn't want to offer any explanations yet. He wanted to see if Himmler had any idea what could have happened there.

"Was there an attack? Perhaps wild animals or grave robbers?" Himmler asked intrigued.

"No, except that our soldiers thought the skeleton bodies were unnatural. No animal can clean the bodies so well in such a short time. They didn't see any living animal close by," Werner replied and stood still by the doorway.

"Unnatural... Supernatural, perhaps?" A spark of interest was now in Himmler's voice. "If that's the case, the groups should look around to see if they can locate the missing archeologists."

"*Jawohl*, SS-Reichsführer," Werner said and left the room.

He barely had time to sit behind his desk when the phone rang again. This time it was Field Marshal Erwin Rommel calling from the Afrikakorps headquarters.

"Someone captured the Zeppelin leaving Cairo and killed our soldiers. I wasn't at the airport. Field Marshal Feder Taffer sacrificed his life there. He was returning to Berlin to report the latest news about Italy and Russia. I sent a couple of my soldiers there to find out what had happened. They found the bodies of all the soldiers and officers slain on the ground, bleeding. No sign of the assailant. The airship won't answer calls."

"I must report this immediately to SS-Reichsführer Heinrich Himmler," Werner replied and ended the call. He walked fast to Himmler's door and knocked. This time he was let in immediately.

"SS-Reichsführer Heinrich Himmler, Field Marshal Erwin Rommel called reporting that several officers and soldiers had died at Cairo airport. Also, the Zeppelin leaving Cairo was stolen. Someone else is onboard and flying it."

"There must be German officers onboard. Why don't they take over?" Himmler asked puzzled.

"Perhaps they are dead too," Werner replied.

Himmler looked furious. "We can't shoot the airship down. If we shoot it and it explodes, we might kill our officers and important business leaders. Find out who had tickets for that flight."

"*Jawohl*, SS-Reichsführer," Werner said and left the room to make the call. He found out soon that several high-ranking officers of different branches were on board, as well as major industry leaders. *This is not good*, Werner thought and went back to Himmler to report his findings.

Himmler let him in and asked, "What did you find out?"

"Carl Bosch of I.G. Farben, Alfried Krupp of Krupp Group, and Friedrich Flick of Flick companies are onboard. Also, several of our officers," Werner listed the familiar names.

"Ach, we can't shoot Farben, Krupp, and Flick. We would lose our industry allies. These men are visionaries delivering us methods to win this war," Himmler said more to himself. "We have to monitor the Zeppelin and find out where it lands." He looked pensive. Werner stood still and waited for more instructions.

"The excavation site and the tomb were near the Valley of the Kings, and everyone was dead on that site. Now, we have the airport where our soldiers and officers are slaughtered. What if these incidents are linked?" Himmler mused.

"Linked?" Werner repeated.

"Yes, what if there is a supernatural power or a tool found in that tomb, and someone is using it to kill the competitors and anyone who stands in his way?" Himmler tapped the table with a pen. "We need to be present when the airship lands. We need that weapon. We would win this war if we had it in our possession," he commented. "Get our best experts to monitor the blimp's route and estimate when it will land."

"*Jawohl,* SS-Reichsführer," Werner greeted and left the room to obey the orders of his superior officer.

The night is turning out to be extremely exciting, Werner thought.

27

Inside the Blimp

While Himmler had discovered what had happened at the excavation site and the airport, the industrialists onboard saw an opportunity. Carl Bosch, Alfried Krupp, and Friedrich Flick huddled together and Carl whispered, "If we could get our hands on the power that young woman has, we would win the war. Her power with our technical know-how would be invincible."

They decided to suggest an alliance between their industry groups and this woman they now knew as Dina. They approached her and stopped politely next to the table.

"We would like to have a word with this young lady," Carl Bosch of I.G. Farben said, and when Dina turned her face to him, he introduced himself and the others. "I'm Carl Bosch of I.G. Farben, and my colleagues are Alfried Krupp of Krupp Group and Friedrich Flick of Flick Companies. You might have heard of our companies."

Dina waited for Lillian to translate. Her face remained unemotional, and she didn't reply.

Jack said, "She does not know any companies in our world. She is not from this time. She is ancient. If you want to suggest something, then just say it. She can then decide if she's interested or not. Remember, she is from the pharaoh's time, and nothing in this world is familiar to her. Even the words describing the new companies and technologies are strange. Lillian has a hard time translating anything modern to the ancient language."

Carl Bosch nodded. He pulled a chair and sat down, and his colleagues took a seat at the nearby table, keeping an eye on both Dina and Carl. Carl started, "I want to suggest an alliance between you and our companies. We would make a formidable force in this world." He turned his eyes to Lillian, who translated it to Dina.

Dina raised her eyebrows. "Why would I need an alliance with anyone? When I find the scarab, I will rule all the living world, and you will all be my slaves."

Jack chuckled when Lillian translated that to Carl Bosch, and his face showed disappointment.

"You will need assistance." Carl frowned.

"I don't need any assistance except those who will help me find the scarab and then translate my wishes," Dina said haughtily.

Carl asked, "What is this scarab?"

Lillian explained, "It's a heart scarab buried with his father. We think it's somewhere in Berlin because we found a German cigarette inside the tomb where her father, Thutmose, was buried. That's the reason we are hurrying to Berlin."

"Ach! I see," Carl said. "How do you know it's in Berlin?"

"We don't. We had to tell her something because otherwise, she would have killed us. It could be anywhere in Germany or wherever the German archeologists took it," Jack replied, and added, "If Dina finds out that she does not need you, she will kill you immediately, so you better be useful or pretend to be helpful if you want to live another hour or so."

"Then perhaps we can help. We have contacts in many museums, and it will be faster to find the scarab with our influence," Carl replied. "As you know, the German soldiers and archeologists have absconded with many artifacts and taken them to various places. A scarab sounds important and could also be in our leader's possession."

Lillian translated the wish to Dina, who nodded. "I will accept your offer to help."

"Then it is settled. Let me discuss where the scarab could be with my colleagues, and then we'll make a list of possible places," Carl replied and stood up and talked with the other industrialists.

"What will they get in return?" Jack asked.

Lillian asked the same question from Dina.

Dina replied, "They will stay alive."

28

Dina's New Allies

Dina was still not accustomed to this new world with new transportation and clinging clothes. The fabrics were coarser than what she used to wear, and the jewelry looked cheap compared to her golden armbands, rings, and necklaces in the past.

She did not completely trust Lillian, who translated for her, but she also realized that when the world had changed so much, it was difficult for her to find the words to describe tools, events, weapons, and other technology.

She trusted that Lillian and Jack were afraid of her and, thus, would do as she requested.

Now, her interest was piqued because the four men had suggested a pact between her and them.

She realized that her power was alluring to the men. With her power, these men could rule the country, win a war, and kill their enemies. Why would she want to give them that power? No reason for her to do that unless she would get her hands on the heart scarab. If they could assist in finding it, she would spare their lives and perhaps give them a position in her kingdom.

Carl Bosch, Alfried Krupp, and Friedrich Flick glanced at each other after Dina had said she would let them keep their lives. Carl asked, "Surely if we do you a favor, you will repay us?"

"Isn't your life enough?" Dina asked, raising her eyebrows. Her black eyes bored into Carl, who had voiced the question.

"*Natürlich*!" Carl said and raised his hands in front of her palms toward Dina. "Calm down. We will find out where the scarab is."

Jack commented, "If you need another demonstration of her power, I'm sure she will be happy to show you, or you can contact Cairo and ask what is left of your soldiers at the airport. I'm sure someone has found the remains by now."

Carl swallowed loudly. "It seems it's in all our interest to find this scarab and fast."

"Yes, except we don't know where it is. Her father, Thutmose, was buried in the Tombs of Nobles. We found his gravesite." Lillian added,

"Dina has less than two days left, and we don't know what will happen then."

Jack poured some more wine into Lillian's glass, took the whiskey bottle, poured a generous drink to himself, and offered it to the Germans. "What would help is if you could find out who visited the tomb and took the artifacts from there."

Carl leaned back on his chair. "You said you found a German cigarette there, meaning it had to have been a recent find."

"Yes, I'd say so. There was no dust over it," Jack replied. "I thought it had been left there recently."

"I had not heard any news of Thutmose's tomb being found and artifacts discovered," Lillian added. "I follow the archeological news, and I would have heard if it had been announced in research news. I checked all the news before we left London a couple of weeks ago, and I don't remember any mention of Thutmose in any recent discoveries."

"Our archeologists Walther Wolfe and Carl Manheim had discovered a new tomb site, and that's the most recent discovery," Alfried Krupp commented. "I talked about the archeological treasures with the SS *Obergruppenführer* at the airport before we embarked on this aircraft. He was excited that the archeologists had found an untouched tomb near the Valley of the Kings."

Lillian sighed. "They found Dina there. Both the German archeologists are dead."

"Yes, but they must have sent their previous discoveries to Berlin. Berlin headquarters required a detailed catalog of what has been found and where. Walther Wolfe was very meticulous. He must have sent the artifacts of this other tomb before he went to the site where he was killed," Alfried commented. "I know he was in Egypt before that tomb. He visited the Valley of the Kings and Theban Necropolis before starting to excavate in this new unopened tomb area."

Carl Bosch nodded, agreeing. "Ah, yes. Walther Wolfe was the chief archeologist, so it would make sense that he was there and ordered the crew to open the tombs in Theban Necropolis. If anyone has the heart scarab, then it would be him."

"We need to find out what Walther Wolfe discovered in the tomb," Lillian said, looking pensive. "How difficult would it be to get the list of artifacts from the headquarters?"

Carl took a drink and glanced at Dina, who sat unmoving, staring outside at the night sky. "I can get the list. It's in Himmler's office. I need to make a call to his assistant."

"Could you send a message from the cockpit?" Jack asked.

"We can try." Carl Bosch stood up and headed to the cockpit. Jack got up a bit unsteadily because of his drinking and said, "I better go there too. Sawyer doesn't know we are working together now."

Lillian nodded. She decided it was time to explain what the Germans had said to Dina. She explained it to her so that she thought they were being helpful.

The pilot contacted Himmler's headquarters, asking for a list of artifacts found in Egypt in Theban Necropolis. He asked it to be delivered to the Berlin airport where they would be landing.

After Carl Bosch's call was made, he waited for the answer. He knew they would need permission or confirmation from Himmler or his assistant.

29

In Berlin

Werner Grothman got the message that Bosch had contacted from the zeppelin and also what he had asked. He quickly walked to inform Himmler about the recent contact.

Himmler rubbed his temples and said, "It seems that our industrialists are still alive and possibly in charge. That's good. Let our troops know that no one is to shoot the Zepp arriving from Cairo. Let it land as scheduled."

"What about the list he asked?" Werner Grothman asked.

"Let me look at the list first to see what would interest them. I believe something important is on the list, and that's why the airship is heading this way. We need to find out what it is before they land. We must have missed something when the artifacts of the previous excavations and tombs were cataloged," Himmler replied and turned his eyes back to the paperwork ahead of him.

Werner Grothman left Himmler's office and went to look for the inventory list. He got it in his hands and returned to Himmler, who read it and frowned. "Nothing seems to stand out. Nothing extraordinary. Nothing that would contain supernatural powers. What is it that they are after?"

"Could it be a part of an object, and then the power is released when put together?" Werner Grothman suggested.

Himmler read the inventory list again. It seemed to be a list of jewelry, sarcophaguses, ceramic pots, and small statues made of gold. *Could it have something to do with the sarcophaguses? They were not opened. They assumed they would have mummies inside. They had wanted to wait for Chief Archeologist Walther Wolfe to return from his trip to Egypt and continue examining them. We won't know the answer before they land,* Himmler thought, frustrated. *However, the good news is that the industrialists seem to be in charge of the aircraft.*

"Did Carl Bosch mention what had happened inside the aircraft?" Himmler asked.

His assistant replied, "No, he only requested the inventory list to be delivered to the airport." So, they still didn't know what the fate of their officers was onboard.

"Make sure we have our troops waiting for the stolen Zeppelin at the airport when it lands. I want the passengers to be contained and find out if intruders are inside," Himmler ordered.

"*Jawohl,* SS-Reichsführer," Werner Grothman replied and greeted him with the usual Nazi greeting before leaving the room and delivering the orders to the SS-troops.

30

Landing in Berlin

Meanwhile, Dina was getting anxious. She thought the flight was too slow. He glanced outside, gestured to her remaining mummies, and mumbled something. The mummies grabbed the ropes and started pulling the zeppelin forward. The wind grew stronger, and soon it was storm-level.

Lillian noticed Dina's moves and her quiet words. She remembered how Dina had manipulated the winds when they were looking for Thutmose's tomb on the burial site of the noblemen and the priests opposite Luxor in Egypt. Back then, Dina had commanded the wind to stop. Now it seemed she had done the opposite. Lillian nudged Jack, who was drunk, and his head lolled against the back of the chair. "I'm going to the cockpit." She stood up and walked to the front of the blimp.

She opened the door, and Sawyer and the co-pilot glimpsed at Lillian. "What's going on?" Sawyer asked and pointed at the mummies, who were now in front of the Zeppelin pulling the aircraft in the storm toward their destination. "This is incredible. The speed is triple compared to a normal airship speed. And this looks more like a hearse now that the mummies are pulling it."

"Dina. She made the wind. I think she's unhappy with how slow we traveled. She wants to reach our destination faster. I saw her gesturing to the mummies and ordering them." Lillian grabbed the doorframe as the zeppelin swayed in the strong wind.

"Do we need to be in the cockpit, or is this aircraft flying by itself?" Sawyer asked with a cranky voice.

"You better direct it. I don't know if Dina or the mummies know which way Berlin is," Lillian replied. "If you want to take a break, you can because Dina is making sure nothing gets in our way."

"Sure, I could stretch my legs and have a snack and a drink," Sawyer replied and got up. The co-pilot glanced at him. "Are you sure we both can go?"

"Yes, I believe so. Dina has taken the reins, and the mummies are pulling this Zeppelin to Berlin," Sawyer replied, following Lillian to the dining room.

The next hours went much the same way until finally, they reached the German borders and saw few lights under them.

Berlin was dark with no lights because the Germans didn't want the Allies to bomb them.

It was almost sunrise, and the sky was lighter blue when the airship reached Berlin.

The co-pilot was worried. "I don't want to blow up in the air. I don't know if the mummies can handle landing this blimp. I'd like for us to do it instead."

"Okay, I'll go talk to our resident devil." Sawyer left the cockpit to talk to Dina. "Could you let us land the aircraft, please?"

Lillian translated his request dutifully, and Dina nodded. She waved her hand, and the wind calmed down, and the mummies returned to the side of the zeppelin, hanging there by the ropes.

"Thank you," Sawyer said and returned to the cockpit with his copilot.

Meanwhile, Himmler had entrusted his top SS officer, Helmut Schmidt, with the critical task of receiving the hijacked airship upon its arrival. Helmut, a man in his thirties with a rounded face, blond hair cut short, and thick-framed glasses, belied his unassuming appearance with a reputation as a skilled investigator and interrogator. His demeanor was more akin to a meticulous accountant than a battle-hardened soldier, but his expertise in extraction and persuasion was unmatched. As the first light of dawn crept over the horizon, Helmut stood poised at the airport, awaiting the blimp's landing. Himmler's warning echoed in his mind: the supernatural entity onboard was an unknown quantity, and he should be ready for anything.

Helmut Schmidt viewed the sky with his binoculars and saw the zeppelin approaching the airfield. Human-like figures hung on the side of it. *Mummies!* he realized. *Himmler was correct. A supernatural power is inside the stolen Zepp guiding it here*, he thought.

The zeppelin approached at a slower speed and landed smoothly on the ground. *It was an excellent landing*, Helmut thought and put down his binoculars. *I should congratulate the pilot, whoever it was.*

He gestured to his soldiers. "*Achtung*! Cairo's airship has landed. Be ready! We might face an enemy or a friend."

The soldiers gathered in front of the airport building and kept their rifles ready to fire.

31

At the Airport

Helmut Schmidt's long black leather trench coat flapped in the wind around his legs as he walked closer to the zeppelin. He stopped near the doorway. He stood still, his hands behind his back. His soldiers stood further back, waiting for his gesture to determine if they needed to fire.

The mummies jumped off first and gathered around the doorway. The airport crew was told not to approach the airship as the ladder was attached to the bottom of the blimp.

Lillian took a coffee pot from the flight attendant. She walked to their table where Jack was snoring, his legs on a chair, his head lolling on his chest. She swung Jack's legs down off the chair where he had kept them. "Time to wake up!"

And a moment later, Lillian slid a coffee cup across the smooth table at Jack, who looked at Lillian, squinting and yawning. "Drink some coffee."

Jack had a bad hangover after drinking so much all night. He drank the coffee and winced. "Is it morning already?"

Lillian replied, "We've landed in Berlin. We need to go."

"Berlin? Already?" Jack asked and brushed his hair with his fingers.

Rolling her eyes, Lillian plastered a smile on her face. "Yes, already."

Jack caught it, holding the mug of swirling the steamy hot black liquid in both hands, enjoying the scent of the fresh coffee. He sat up and poured it into his throat.

"Here's some more coffee," Lillian commented and poured Jack another cup of hot coffee.

Inside the cockpit, the copilot said, "Someone needs to open the door, then the ladder must be attached so that the passengers can get out of the blimp."

Sawyer nodded. "Okay, I will go tell Dina, and she can take care of it. She has the mummy crew ready on the ground. I don't think we'll get any real airport crew to help us because of the mummies and the SS soldiers." He gestured outside to the soldiers standing with their rifles ready and the mummies hovering near the blimp. He left to find Dina in the dining room.

Sawyer nodded to Lillian and instructed, "Have Dina request the mummies prepare the ladder, I'll open the door." With a swift gesture, Dina commanded the mummies to ready the ladder, and Sawyer pushed the door open.

They felt the cold morning air coming through the opened doorway.

The passengers began to disembark, descending the ladder one by one, their movements steady and cautious as they stepped out into the unknown.

The first to leave the Zeppelin were the wives and daughters of the killed officers and the businessmen. They rushed down the ladder toward the soldiers crying for help.

Helmut's composure momentarily faltered as he beheld the distraught group of women and children, their tears and cries piercing the air. His head swiveled back and forth, his eyes scanning the chaotic scene as the passengers rushed past him. A flicker of confusion crossed his face: These aren't the ones with supernatural powers... and they're not British either, he thought, his mind racing with the unexpected turn of events. His gaze snapped back to the airship, his focus intensifying as he searched for the true targets of his mission.

Dina had waited until the other passengers had left, and then she stood up. "Slaves, follow me," she ordered and walked to the doorway.

The mummies saw her and stood still, facing her as she climbed down. Last were the Brits, including Sawyer, and then the German businessmen. The co-pilot and other crewmembers stayed in the blimp. They thought staying behind would be safer than following the monster outside.

Helmut Schmidt noticed the mummies gathering around the ladder when Dina climbed down, her dark brown hair flowing around her shoulders. *Is that the supernatural being?* he thought. *A woman? She doesn't look dangerous...*

Then Dina turned her head and latched her pitch-black eyes on Helmut.

Helmut felt as if he was looking in the fathomless pit, and he was sure he felt an evil staring back at him. A pure evil, not just a maniac or a violent person. Helmut shivered as the hairs on his neck stood up. *This must be the supernatural power Himmler wanted.*

He was sure of it. He took a deep breath, pushed his glasses higher on his nose, and took a few steps forward.

The mummies gathered around Dina now as if protecting her.

Dina stood there still, watching the SS soldiers and the officer coming forward.

The tension was high until Helmut lifted his hand and gestured for the soldiers to lower their guns. The German businessmen came forward. Alfried Krupp stepped next to Dina and asked, "Do you have the inventory list for us?"

Helmut nodded. "Yes, I have it here." He tapped on his breast pocket.

"Can I see it, please?" Alfried asked. He had a high forehead and narrow face, and dark hair.

"Just a moment," Helmut replied. "I'm the highest-ranking officer here. I will give you the commands, not the other way around."

The three German businessmen, Carl Bosch, Alfried Krupp, and Friedrich Flick, approached Helmut and came to stand so close to him that only he could hear their words.

Alfried said, "I must warn you. We've seen with our own eyes what this woman can do. First, she commands the wind. Second, she can kill with one gesture, and third, these mummies follow her orders."

Carl Bosch explained, "She was a man when this trip started. She took the body of the young woman you see in front of you. She is a specter or a demon that possesses the human body and is to be feared and obeyed. Don't throw your weight around. She won't tolerate it. We saw what happened to the officers onboard and at the airport where we left."

Helmut squinted his eyes and looked in Dina's direction, unsure of what to believe. *This all sounds unbelievable. How could this person be all that these businessmen claim she is? I know these businessmen to be clever, ruthless even. They would not lie. They would not dare to cross Himmler,* he thought.

"And these Brits, are they also protected by this woman?" Helmut asked.

"She calls them her slaves," Alfried replied. "In ancient Egypt, she was a noblewoman because her father was a high priest. She's used to having servants and slaves."

"How did she wake up? What are her intentions?" Helmut asked, frowning.

"I would rather ask the key question: Can we get her on our side in this war? She has incredible powers. We could win the war easily if she were with us. She would be a formidable ally," Carl Bosch replied and pushed his hands into his pockets.

"Ach, I know. Himmler is excited about the possibilities of having this kind of power on our side," Helmut replied and glanced at Dina, who started looking impatient.

"Show me the list. I need to know what was found in Thutmose's tomb," Carl said.

Helmut pulled out the inventory list and handed it to him.

Carl viewed it, then took it to Lillian. "This is the inventory. Is there anything here that could be the scarab? Perhaps, it's named differently."

Lillian took the list and viewed it. "A sarcophagus, a mummy, pots and pans, some statues... No, I don't see the heart stone mentioned." She turned to Dina and asked, "The tomb contents do not mention the scarab. Could it be wrapped inside the mummy or hidden in the sarcophagus?"

Dina faced Lillian and said, "It's possible. I need to see them. Where are they?"

Lillian translated the question to Carl, who shook his head. "I don't know. I need to ask if that officer knows. I only got the list from him." Carl strolled back to Helmut, asked the question, and then returned to Lillian. "He said they are in the warehouse next to Neues museum, which is currently closed."

"Can we go there now?" Lillian asked. "Dina is in a hurry and wants to get her hands on the items found in her father's tomb."

"What will happen if she doesn't find it?" Carl asked quietly.

"She'll kill us. She was given a specific timeframe to find it. I don't know what will happen if she does not find it before that," Lillian replied. "I know if we don't help her, she will find someone else, and our lives will be worth nothing."

"Okay, let's go then." Carl turned and walked to meet Helmut. "We'll go to the warehouse and search for the item she is looking for."

"Is she on our side or not?" Helmut wanted to know.

"We can discuss that when we find the scarab she's looking for," Carl replied and pointed at the cars parked by the airport building. "We'll take those cars over there. All of us will go."

Helmut nodded. "I will come too." He wanted to be there when they entered the warehouse because if any guards were there, the presence of an SS officer would certainly help to get inside the building.

32

Helmut's Mistake

Helmut Schmidt had intended only the Germans and the supernatural being to go with him to the warehouse. When Lillian, Jack, and Sawyer followed them, he shouted, "Halt!" Helmut gestured to his soldiers and commanded, "Take these three to interrogation at the headquarters." The soldiers ran, surrounded the three Brits, and pointed their rifles at them. One of them pushed Jack by the shoulder and said in German, "Walk unless you want to get shot."

They marched forward to the waiting truck. The soldiers gestured for them to climb up, and Jack and Sawyer went in first, held out their hands for Lillian, and pulled her up after them. They sat on a narrow seat and waited as the serious-looking SS soldiers followed them. "This is it," Jack said and viewed the grim truck. "We are in the hands of the enemy."

The soldier who came to sit next to them told them, "Shut up. No talking," but only Sawyer and Lillian understood German enough to know that. They were now prisoners of war.

Dina watched this episode with no emotion. She turned to Alfried and Carl and asked something in her ancient language, but the men could not understand a word of what she said. Dina waited for a second, then murmured something. She turned to make an eye-contact with her mummies, and with a rapid wave of her hand, she motioned them to go after the soldiers.

With their linen-wrapped bodies and empty eye sockets, the mummies rushed after the soldiers who had captured the Brits and attacked them. With screams of pain and terror, limb after limb was ripped from the soldiers' bodies. A few soldiers got their rifles and pistols ready and tried to shoot the mummies, but that didn't stop the undead monsters. They continued their massacre until only torn bodies, a pool of crimson red blood, broken white bones protruding from torn-off limbs, and ripped-off heads with milky white eyes were left around the truck. Only then did the mummies stop the massacre and turn to see if anything else was required of them.

Dina sighed and gestured to Lillian and the others to come back to her. They climbed down from the truck and avoided looking around at the body parts lying on the ground. Lillian looked ashen as she tried to ignore the pool of blood and how it got stuck in her shoes. She walked as fast as she could away from the track.

When they reached Dina, Lillian asked, "Why did you help us?"

"Why not? You're my slaves. You work for me." She turned her icy-cold eyes to Helmut and added, "That man is out of time. He should not have crossed me."

She gestured, and the black beetles emerged from her sleeves and rushed to Helmut, who stood still first, not realizing what the black bugs were. Until the bugs started climbing up his legs and digging under his skin and eating him alive, he screamed as the beetles ate his facial flesh revealing a white bony forehead. He collapsed when the beetles devoured his internal organs, and in seconds his body was gone, and only a skeleton was left under the leather trench coat and the black SS uniform. His skull stared at them with empty eye sockets, and his chin bone rested on his chest as the beetles finished their job and scurried back to their queen.

Lillian turned her head away and dry-heaved.

"Ah, that's a way to deal with problems," Jack said, sighing. "More killing."

33

Enemies or Friends?

The three German businessmen, Carl Bosch, Alfried Krupp, and Friedrich Flick, stared in horror as the SS officer's body was cleaned to the bare bones in seconds. They had never seen anything like that. They had seen what Dina could do with the mummies and how she killed the officers on board, strangling them with mummy wraps but watching someone die this horribly was beyond their imagination.

Friedrich was an aristocratic-looking man with greying hair and a high forehead. He stared at the skeleton that used to be Helmut and then swayed. He had witnessed the massacres of the war, but this was different. He had never seen anyone eaten alive. Alfried grabbed his colleague by the arm and whispered, "Stand still. Don't show her fear."

Friedrich glanced at him, swallowed, and nodded. "*Jawohl*!" he replied quietly. He realized they were at the mercy of this monster who could kill them in seconds with a wave of her hand.

Alfried gave a stern look at Carl Bosch, who nodded. He understood perfectly. They were more prisoners now than allies. Carl and Alfried exchanged a glance, and then Carl nodded toward the Brits and raised his eyebrows. It was a silent question: Should they collaborate with the Brits instead of thinking of them as enemies because the enemy of your opponent is your friend?

Alfried nodded as he understood what Carl meant. They had to find a way to get rid of this monster because she would not let anyone else rule this world but herself. That was clear now. She would not take orders from anyone. They both turned to Friedrich, who also nodded slowly. He knew what they meant.

Dina gestured with her hand for them to follow her as she started walking, and the entourage of mummies followed her to the waiting two Großer Mercedes vehicles and stopped next to them. The German businessmen and the Brits followed slowly after them.

No SS soldiers or officers remained alive, so no one reported what had happened to the SS headquarters.

Meanwhile, Himmler paced restlessly in his office, his anxiety palpable as he awaited news about the mysterious entity within the blimp. His mind raced with the possibilities: could this supernatural force be harnessed as a weapon to turn the tide of the war? The prospect of unlocking such power consumed him, driving his every thought.

From time to time, Himmler glanced at the map of Europe and Africa on his wall and then sat down. He was eager to hear from Cairo's blimp. His loyal officer, Helmut Schmidt, was sent to greet the landing blimp. That was an hour ago. He should have reported back or returned to the headquarters to personally report what he had found out. No report, no Helmut.

He called his assistant and asked, "Any news of the airport?"

"*Nein,* SS-Reichsführer," Werner Grothman replied, standing in front of Himmler's desk.

"Send another team to find out what's causing the delay," Himmler ordered.

"*Jawohl,* SS-Reichsführer!" Werner Grothman saluted with his hand straight ahead and marched out. He gave his order on the phone for a group of five soldiers to go to the airport and find out why Helmut Schmidt had not contacted back yet. He sat back behind his desk. He had a bad feeling about this. He knew Helmut personally, and he was never late for any of his reports. He was the most punctual officer he knew.

Werner Grothman rubbed his eyes. He had not had proper sleep for over twenty-four hours. He had taken a short nap on his desk but still felt tired, and his eyelids were heavy. He was sure he could easily sleep for a couple of days if he had some time off. He loosened his collar with his finger. He took a cigarette pack from his drawer and walked outside to smoke. There was nothing he could do now but try to stay sharp and awake.

Black coffee and cigarettes will have to do for now, he thought. He lit his cigarette and glanced up. The sky was grey with heavy clouds, but it wasn't raining yet. *If it was cloudy and rainy, then the Allies would not try to bomb the city tonight*, he thought. They liked a clear sky, but then occasionally, they had bombed on a cloudy day too. He hoped for heavy rain or fog because those weather conditions would be the only ones when the Allies' bombers would not bother the city.

34

Jack, Sawyer, and the Others

"Wait!" Sawyer said, stopping.

Their small group stopped, and everyone turned to stare at him, even Dina.

"What if there are guards at the warehouse? They won't let a group of civilians inside the warehouse," Sawyer explained. "We don't look trustworthy with dirty clothes. Besides, we are enemies in this country. We have the three German businessmen with us, but I don't know if that will guarantee entry to the warehouse." Sawyer still wore his dirty white shirt and khakis, his tanned, lean face looked tired, and his brown hair was tousled.

The three German businessmen, Carl Bosch, Alfried Krupp, and Friedrich Flick looked at each other and conveyed in German, and then Alfried said in English, "We could take the SS officer's uniform from his skeleton. It's not that dirty or bloody. It has some blood, but the long trench coat will cover most of it. I don't believe anyone will stop an SS officer during a war."

Sawyer nodded. "Jack, get dressed. You're drunk enough that no one will care if you have dirty clothes. They might think you have had a long night celebrating, and thus, you're not in your finest and cleanest clothes this morning."

"I'm not drunk enough to wear those clothes," Jack muttered but walked to the skeleton and picked up the uniform, the black leather boots, and the trench coat.

"Officers have hangovers. You look the part," Sawyer insisted.

Groaning, Jack Stiller hurried behind the truck left at the airport by the soldiers, took off his pants, and pulled on the SS officer's pants. They were short, but he put on his boots, and no one would notice anything off. Then he put on the uniform jacket and hat and lastly, the black leather trench coat. He even had a luger on his belt's holster. *Good*, he thought. *It might come in handy*. He marched out from behind the truck and asked, "How do I look?"

"You'll do just fine. Don't speak English. You're a German officer now," Lillian reminded him.

"Yeah, I know," Jack replied, sticking his tongue out of his mouth, and marched with long strides to the cars where the others were already sitting.

Sawyer was sitting behind the driver's seat of the first Mercedes, wearing an SS soldier's jacket and a helmet that he had picked up from one of the dead soldiers, and he greeted Jack when he walked and sat next to him. Dina and Lillian sat behind them. The German businessmen had taken the other car and waited impatiently. Because Jack was an officer, he was not expected to drive.

"Who will drive the mummies in a truck?" Jack asked. Lillian translated to Dina, and with her instructions, one of the mummies got dressed in a soldier's uniform.

The mummies followed in a truck, and the one dressed as a soldier drove it. The helmet was down on his face so no one would notice he was not a real person. Dina gestured for him to follow the two other cars. The three cars moved slowly past the airport building and then headed toward the center of the city.

It was a grey morning, and the low-hanging clouds threatened rain later that day. There was a weekday morning look on the tree-lined avenues in mid-city. The weekends were quieter but during the weekdays, more patrols were on the streets. The pin-oak trees had dark, lush foliage.

Early morning's slow auto traffic and a scarcity of pedestrians on the sidewalks would soon change when the people left their homes to go to work. The coffee shops were just opening, but other businesses were still closed. Small trucks with machine guns at the ready, manned by helmeted soldiers manned small trucks with machine guns drove by, but when they saw the officer's uniform, they greeted them and let them drive by. Some trucks were parked at intersections, checking out the early morning drivers and pedestrians.

The pedestrians kept looking at the sky cynically, viewing the passing airplanes and guessing if they were German planes or enemy fighters because either one might fly that early in the morning. No sirens alerted the citizens of an enemy bombing, so it seemed to be a quiet day ahead.

35

The Warehouse

An open truck of grey uniformed soldiers drove slowly by. They did not seem to care about the two black Mercedes vehicles with the SS officer, the German businessmen, or the truck with the mummy driver.

Driving through the quiet streets of Berlin that early morning made Sawyer think about their future. He wished he could converse with Jack and Lillian without Dina listening and asking to translate everything they said. Sawyer wondered if this quietness was only because of the brewing storm as if the Germans were playing down the ongoing war. It was the late summer of 1940, and the war efforts were heightened, but it seemed that the Berliners' daily routines were not affected too much by the ongoing war in Europe.

Finally, the neoclassical museum building loomed ahead. Sawyer drove to the east façade of the museum and parked. Alfried, who drove the other vehicle, soon stopped next to him and pointed to the left.

"The warehouse is that building. It does not look like a warehouse but more like an office building, but Neues Museum uses it for extra storage space for the artifacts shipped from the archeological excavations all over the world." He took out the inventory list from his pocket, glanced at it one more time, and added, "The shipment from Cairo should be on the basement level when we go in."

Both cars and the truck parked in front of the grey-stone building. As they had suspected, a couple of guards were standing by, but when they saw the fearsome-looking SS officer's uniform, they didn't ask much and let them pass. Only one elderly man sat in a wooden chair by the doorway, reading a newspaper. He glanced at them when they opened the door. He had a tuft of white hair on top of his head and a stooping figure. When he saw the SS uniform, he quickly rose from his chair.

"Good morning," Jack said in his best German. "We are here to find some Egyptian artifacts. They are stored on the basement level. Can you point us the right way?" He tried to sound haughty and superior.

"It's that door over there," the old man pointed at the door by the end of the dim hallway.

"Thank you," Jack nodded and proceeded in front of the group to the door.

The old man looked curiously as the strange entourage walked past him. He didn't ask any questions because the SS officer and the soldier were with them.

Jack fumbled for the side of the door for a light switch but didn't find it. Then he reached his hand up and found a string and pulled it. A cheap light bulb lit, and a yellowish light illuminated the stairway. The light was weak and created long shadows when they descended the spiraling staircase slowly and carefully. When they got to the bottom level, Jack reached to light the next light bulb and pulled the string. It only lit the small area. They saw rows and rows of wooden crates of different sizes in front of them, some had tarps over them, and some were open with straw inside. A narrow path was left between the wooden crates piled high above their heads. The employees had left the ladders by the wall for easier access to the higher crates.

"How will we find anything here?" Lillian asked, frustrated. She craned her neck and glimpsed up. "These crates reach the ceiling!"

"Did the inventory list mention where the items from Cairo could be?" Sawyer asked.

Alfried pulled the list from his pocket and checked. "Yes, it mentions 2/4. If that means anything to anyone."

"It could be a second row and fourth crate," Jack mumbled. "Or it could mean the second crate and fourth crate upward."

"Let's start checking the boxes, and maybe we can find a clue about how these are cataloged," Lillian suggested. She didn't mind using more time because she knew Dina had limited time on Earth. She didn't know what would happen to her, but she hoped Anubis would take Dina back to where she came from.

36

One Day Gone, Two Left

Dina stared at the wall where her own shadow with the jackal head was growing, moving, growling.

Sawyer saw it first and stopped, staring at it. The others soon noticed that the shadows grew larger, the basement area dimmed, and the atmosphere became more ominous. The temperature dropped to chilling, and they all felt a cold breeze blow through the basement.

Dina shivered as if someone had touched her with icy fingers.

The shadow with the jackal head grew until it reached the ceiling. "Dina!" the shadow called her name. The gusty wind blew through the warehouse when the ancient being spoke. His voice echoed in the walls. His figure grew larger, engulfing the ceiling and reaching the next wall. A low murmur, like a jackal growling, sounded inside the basement.

Shivering, Dina swallowed loudly, and her hand went to her throat as if she was having difficulty breathing.

The shadows on the floor morphed into human-looking figures with see-through heads, arms, and legs. They crawled and slid towards her, gathering around her. Their transparent hands grabbed her ankles, their fingers reached up her legs, clutching onto her, hands strong like they were bones and claws instead of made of shadows. They kept pulling her down to the floor to come with them to the shadow world, the world of the dead. Dina struggled and tried to stand upright, but the creatures were powerful, and they got her to kneel. She leaned forward, but they kept pulling her with more force. More and more of these beings appeared from the shadows of the basement, moving toward her.

"No!" Dina cried and ripped herself away from the shadow hands. "You promised me seventy-two hours."

The jackal-head god Anubis moved away from the wall and stepped forward, now fully human, and his face came within inches of Dina's when he replied, "Yes, one day is gone, two left." His eyes burned red, his sharp canine teeth snapped inches away from Dina's face, and she could smell the carnivore's breath.

Anubis gestured with his hand, and the shadowy bodies withdrew back to the shadows of the room and disappeared. He stood still, viewing the group around Dina, and said, "I'm Anubis, and soon you will all be mine."

He disappeared back into the shadows as swiftly and quietly as he had appeared.

"Ahh-choo!" Jack's loud sneeze sent a cloud of dust up into the air around us and startled everyone.

Everyone turned to face Jack, even Dina. She was still paler than usual, but the normal sound of sneezing seemed to wake her up from the terror Anubis had caused. Dina inhaled deeply, holding her hand on her chest, and rubbed her neck. She glanced around at the shadows fearing to see more ethereal figures, but they were all gone. The basement looked just as before. Anubis had just warned Dina, not taken her away from this world. Regardless, Dina felt like she couldn't move and that her feet were stuck on the floor because of the fear of God Anubis.

"Sorry! I couldn't help it," Jack said and rubbed his nose, desperately trying to stop the annoying and persistent tickle that would result in another loud sneeze. "It's so dusty and cold down here," he said apologetically.

The others relaxed and seemed to breathe more easily. The ancient god was gone, and everything was back to normal: a damp basement and Jack sneezing.

Jack leaned forward and then sneezed in Lillian's face. "Ah, sorry about that."

Lillian wiped her face with her handkerchief and huffed. "Jack! For God's sake. Behave! And use a handkerchief next time!"

"I couldn't help it. Too dusty with all this straw and old mummy wraps," Jack muttered and sniffed.

Lillian frowned and turned her back on him, thinking, *Now we know the deadline.* Anubis had just told them. Two more days and Anubis would take her back to the shadow world if she failed to find the heart scarab that belonged to Thutmose. She glimpsed at Sawyer, who nodded quietly. He had also noticed the timeline. Her eyes moved to the German businessmen, and they also lifted their chins almost invisibly to acknowledge the importance of Anubis's visit.

Lillian's eyes moved to Dina, who was still lost in her thoughts, her fingers fiddling her throat as if she felt the pressure of Anubis's words still there. Dina didn't look as assertive as before. The appearance of the ancient God had scared her.

Lillian wondered if the mummies waiting for them outside in the truck were still there or did Anubis take them with him. She had no answer. Dina had not told the mummies to follow her inside the warehouse. They might still be out there.

37

More Mummies

Dina moved forward, looking at the rows of open crates and closed boxes, and ordered, "Slaves, find my father's sarcophagus." She was no less threatening now than before Anubis' appearance. She didn't show any emotion when she viewed the basement and the task ahead.

Lillian noticed that Dina's hands were shaking. *Anubis scared Dina even if she did not show it much,* she thought.

"The numbers 2/4," Jack started, "we could check the second row first and then the fourth box up."

Everyone else nodded, and Jack proceeded to the row to his right. He counted the second row, then the boxes upwards. "No, it's not this. There are only three boxes up," he said.

"Maybe it's the second box from the doorway and the fourth up?" Sawyer suggested and walked back to the first row, chose the second pile of crates, and viewed it. "This one is an open crate. There's no boxes or crates above it."

Lillian frowned. She leaned down and looked closely at the tags on the crates. Each had a specific list on the side. "This first one is seven / one," she said." She walked to the next one and said, "This is seven / two."

Jack said slowly, "So, if the numbers start from the seven, then the smaller ones must be on the back of the warehouse." He walked with long strides to the back of the large hall, then checked the last crate. "This is number one here." He walked to the next row. "This is two." He glanced up. Four crates were piled on top of each other. "It could be the top one," Jack said. "How do we get it down?"

Dina had followed the group to the back, and Lillian told her what Jack thought the right box was. Dina gestured with her hands and muttered something.

The crates with sarcophaguses or mummies started moving. They heard pounding as if someone alive was opening the box from inside. They watched as the crate's lid above them was pushed outwards, and a mummy sat up. He was not the only one; they saw ten other mummies climbing down from their crates and gathering on the walkway between the crates.

"I'm not sure this was helpful," Jack said, scratching his head. "Now we have plenty of mummies alive, but is one of them Dina's father?"

Dina stood still. She spoke strange words in an ancient language, and one of the mummies moved forward.

Lillian whispered. "I think she is calling her father to come forward. That might be him."

The mummy of Dina's father was in good condition. The wraps were intact. Some other mummies had more worn-out and yellowed wraps. *Perhaps, that is due to the pristine condition of Dina's father's tomb, and because he was a nobleman*, Lillian thought as she assessed the mummies gathering around them. Now, she could count twenty altogether.

Dina spoke to her mummy-father and asked where the scarab was.

The mummy pointed to the sarcophagus he had left open in the crate. Dina pointed at the other mummies and ordered, "Get that sarcophagus down."

The mummies followed her orders and climbed on each side of the crates, grabbed the sarcophagus, and lowered it down, where several other mummies took it and placed it on the floor in front of Dina.

Dina kneeled and patted through the inside of the sarcophagus from top to bottom. Nothing was there. Her face turned furious. "It's not here." She turned her face to Lillian, who shrugged. "We found your father and the sarcophagus. The heart scarab should be here."

At that moment, Alfried interrupted. “Yes, that’s correct, unless the chief archeologist decided to send a special token to our chancellor Adolph Hitler.” He turned to others and explained, “The archeologists sent gifts to our leader because they wanted to fund their next trips. If this heart scarab looked valuable and interesting, the chief archeologist might have shipped it separately to our Führer.”

“I don’t believe this,” Jack muttered and leaned against the boxes. “Now we need to go after Hitler too?”

“It’s possible. That’s what I think happened,” Alfried said and glanced at the other Germans, who nodded vigorously.

Lillian quickly translated what the German businessman had told them.

“We need to get it back,” Dina said sternly. “I must have it.”

She marched past the group back to the stairway. The others followed her one after another. What else could they do?

“What about the mummies?” Lillian asked. The mummies stood hovering in the middle of the floor, unsure if they should come with them.

“They can come with us. They might be of use,” Dina replied and gestured to the mummies to follow.

38

Dina's Fear

Dina looked warily at the end of the hallway and the stairs. That was where Anubis had appeared to her. She shivered. She walked slowly, glancing at the shadows making sure they were not moving or trying to grab her. When she got to the stairs, she quickly ran up, then sighed in relief. She had walked by the scary area and not been caught.

The lobby's guard was on his break. He was an elderly man with snow-white hair and a wrinkled white shirt, and he had suspenders holding his pants up. He had put away his newspaper and had taken out his lunch: a thermos pint bottle filled with hot coffee and the workman's lunch kit, inside of which he had sandwiches and some tuna for the cat.

The guard's cat had been lying on his feet, and when he sensed he would get some food, he started twining around his legs. The guard patted the cat's back and gave his little tabby cat a bowl of milk and a bit of fish to eat. The cat went to his bowl eagerly, but his lunch was soon interrupted.

When the cat sensed Dina, he turned and glared at her, and her back arched, his tail held out stiff and straight, and he hissed and spat at Dina. He ignored his tuna and milk even though he was hungry, and they were his favorite food.

"What is it, Tabby?" the guard asked, surprised, trying to reach the cat, but he clearly didn't want to be distracted. He stared at Dina, flattening his ears against his head, crouching low, and curling his tail under him. He feared Dina but also wanted to show his owner that he knew who the real danger was, namely Dina.

Dina backed against the wall. She feared cats, as the ancient world believed cats could see inside human souls, and Dina knew she was no longer a human. Also, cats were magical creatures, and the gods had the power to transform themselves into cats' bodies. She thought this cat was just another trick by Anubis.

"No!" she cried. "I have time. You promised seventy-two hours!" She held her hand in her throat, fearing someone would appear from the cat's body and take her life away.

The others came up from the basement after her and noticed her fear.

Lillian passed Dina first and looked at the cat. She turned to Dina and said, "It's just a cat."

"It's a horrible creature," Dina whispered, pressing herself against the wall.

The guard saw a terrified woman and said, "It's my kitty cat. Usually, he's a well-behaved cat and doesn't cause any harm. I don't know why he acts like this now."

Sawyer commented quietly, "A smart cat. He knows who the devil is."

The guard tried to grab the cat, but he wouldn't move. He stood still like an angry statue and kept hissing.

"Please, go," he said, pointing at the door. "He will calm down when you leave. He might have just gotten scared because we don't see many visitors in this place."

Lillian nodded and walked to the door, followed by her brother, Sawyer, and the German businessmen. Dina watched them carefully, withdrew from the wall, and ran to the doorway.

The cat tried to jump on her, but the guard grabbed him by the collar and held him. "No, you can't attack our guests. Bad cat!" the guard told his cat.

Outside, Dina leaned on the wall and shivered. She stood there for a while to calm down.

A flaw in our demon, Jack thought. *Our Dina fears cats.*

39

Where to Go Next?

Sawyer approached Lillian casually and whispered, "Can we use Dina's fear of cats somehow?"

"I don't know. Perhaps. We'll need to see what opportunities we get," Lillian replied.

They moved away from each other. Jack saw that and came to Lillian and asked quietly, "What did Sawyer want from you?"

"Nothing." Lillian shrugged and walked away.

Jack squinted his eyes. He didn't like Sawyer near his sister. Who knew what they were planning? He shoved his hands in his pockets and stared sullenly at Sawyer, his curly hair carelessly on his forehead, easy smile, and tall figure.

Alfried and the other two German businessmen were together conversing in German. Jack moved to stand next to them and asked, "Have you figured out something useful?"

Alfried turned to him and replied, "Possibly. We think it's possible that Martin Borman, our leader's right hand, could have taken the scarab with some other valuables from the shipment. The second choice is that our leaders' personal antique dealer Martin Leitch might have been interested in some of the artifacts and taken the scarab with him. The third choice is that our beloved leader has it in his personal art gallery."

Jack shivered as if a cold hand had touched his spine. "What you said inside was only partly true. The scarab could have been gifted to Hitler, or it could be in the hands of the other Nazis. " None of those are good choices," he said, adding, "We can't march into Hitler's home, or to Borman's residence, or even to his art dealer's place."

"Yes, that's the problem," Alfried replied. "We don't know how to proceed from here. We hoped the scarab would be here, but it seems someone has removed it, and it must have happened after the crates were brought here and cataloged at Himmler's office. We can only think of the three I mentioned to you."

Friedrich Flick of Flick Industries nodded vigorously.

Carl Bosch of Bosch Companies said, "Yes, we have no idea which one might have taken the scarab. I expect it is valuable looking, and if the heart scarab is made of a jewel or is full twenty-four karat gold, then I'm sure it would look like a great present to gift to our leader. That's why our first suggestion was that it's in our leader's possession. But now that we've reconsidered, there are two other possibilities."

Jack rubbed his face with his hands. This was worse than what he had expected. They had three choices, and all of them were top Nazis. None of them would be easy to approach.

Lillian and Sawyer walked to their little group and asked, "What's going on?"

Jack waved his hand in front of the Germans and said, "I'll let them tell you."

The Germans explained what they considered had happened to the scarab.

Dina leaned against the wall, surrounded by the mummies. She kept her eyes on them, and finally, when she thought they had conversed long enough, she called Lillian to explain what they were talking about.

Lillian returned to Dina and explained as well as she could in an ancient language.

Dina thought about the problems and said, "We can drive by the houses where these three men live. My father can sense whether his heart scarab is inside the house." She gestured to one of the mummies, who was her father, risen from the underworld.

"Oh, okay," Lillian said. "We should go then." She waved at the men and shouted, "Let's go."

When the men came closer, she explained, "Dina thinks her father can sense if the scarab is inside a building. We might find it if we drive by the locations where these three men reside."

"That's a plan," Sawyer said and climbed back into the driver's seat. He still had his SS soldier's uniform on, and Jack wore the officer's uniform. He waited for the others to get seated. "Where did the mummy go?"

Dina pointed up.

Sawyer leaned out the window and saw Dina's mummy-father lying on top of the car. "I wonder what the other drivers will say when they see that," Sawyer mumbled and started the car.

This time Jack was driving with the Germans. He didn't mind. He'd rather travel with them than with Dina.

Sawyer followed him with Dina, Lillian, and the mummy-father on top of the car. The mummy truck was the last of their entourage.

40

Driving Around Berlin

Sawyer asked, "Do you know what Borman's address is?"

"We'll follow Jack. I'm sure the German businessmen know where he can be found, his residence or place of employment," Lillian replied, brushing her hair with her fingers.

This adventure had been stressful. She had napped in the blimp, but the constant stress and fear made her fidgety. She wasn't sure if the German businessmen knew where to find Borman, but anything would help when they needed to stay alive for another forty-eight hours. What happened after that was another problem. She had given it some thought and believed that Dina would return to the underworld.

The mummy hanging on top of the car made the other drivers and pedestrians stare at them. Most pedestrians stopped, and some drivers swerved from their lane when they gawked at the strange sight and hit the cars on the other side.

Sawyer glimpsed back at them and shook his head. "Like they've never seen a mummy before."

Jack drove the car ahead with the German businessmen. Because he wore the uniform of an SS officer, he had no trouble getting past the few army checkpoints around the city with wooden street barricades blocking off parts of the city. When they noticed his black uniform, the soldiers gestured for Jack to drive through. Jack told them in German, "The next car and the truck are part of my entourage." Then he officially saluted them with his right hand and pressed the gas.

"Where do we go?" Jack asked Alfried.

The businessman looked pensive. "First, I would pass Reich Chancellery around the corner on Voßstraße, a western branch off of Wilhelmstraße. If the heart scarab is there, then the mummy in the next car will alert us," Alfried replied, turning his head to check out the mummy following them on top of the second vehicle.

"Okay, I've been to Berlin a few times before the war, but I don't know the roads well. You need to instruct where to go," Jack replied glancing over his shoulder. The chaos on the streets caused by the sight of the mummy on top of the second car was visible.

Jack sighed. *What did I get into this time? I should have stayed back in London and enjoyed my life instead of going to an archeological excavation with Lillian. This was my worst decision ever!*

Jack's thoughts were not so different from Lillian's in the next vehicle, sitting with Dina. She had no idea what to do with the demon next to her or how to get rid of Dina. So far, she had come up empty. Her best choice seemed to be to stay alive for the next forty-eight hours and then find out if Dina would vanish. She hoped Dina would not get upset with them before that.

Lillian's eyes surveyed the streets and the building. Only the air war showed its touches: bomb holes in buildings and a crashed British bomber in the park. Lillian took a deep breath when she saw the familiar red-white-blue bull's eye roundel painted on the side of the plane, and the plane's nose art pictured a woman called Eva. The pilot might have survived if the plane had landed in the park. Now the plane was a constant attraction to children as they walked by. Lillian wondered if the pilot was now in the hands of the Gestapo and being questioned and tortured. *If I ever get back to London, I will tell them that the plane looked intact and the pilot might have survived the crash*, she thought.

Jack drove on and soon saw the white building with a long courtyard. "Is that where Hitler is?"

Alfried replied, “Yes, the old building with the courtyard used to be the residence of an aristocrat, Prince Antoni Radziwill, in the late nineteenth century.”

He pointed at the newer building and said, “The new entrance to the New Reich Chancellery is on Voßstraße. “The new building is quite impressive inside. It was finished early this year.” Alfried added, “Many diplomatic events have been held there this year. I visited there a few times. The gallery is said to be longer than the Hall of Mirrors at Versailles.”

When the two vehicles and the truck got closer to the chancellery building, Alfried commented, “You don’t have to drive to the other side. We’ll just drive slowly by and see if anything catches the mummy-father’s attention.”

“Well, let’s hope so. We can’t be driving too slow past this building. We’ll alert all the soldiers at the gate,” Jack said and nodded to the guarding soldiers. He greeted them as he drove by and told them the same thing as the previous soldiers. The soldiers let them all pass by. Jack viewed the rearview mirror and kept his eyes on the mummy. No movement yet.

Lillian poked her head out of the car, called to the soldiers, pointed at the roof of her car, and said in German, “It’s an advertisement for the new Egyptian exhibition at the museum. We’re taking the mummy around the city and then back to the museum.”

The soldiers relaxed and laughed at them, gesturing at the mummy.

Sawyer sighed in relief. “I hope they bought your story.”

"It seems so." Lillian glanced at Dina and asked, "The chancellor's home is here. The mummy does not seem to be moving. Do you think that the scarab is not here?"

Dina said, "The mummy will alert if he senses the scarab. If he's not moving, it's not here."

The two cars and the truck passed the Reich Chancellery and drove on.

"Next, I guess, is Borman's residence," Jack commented.

"Yes, I would think so, unless—" Alfried stopped in the middle of the sentence, then quickly conversed with his friends, tapped Jack on the shoulder, and said, "Could you drive by Himmler's headquarters? We want to make sure no one took anything out of the shipment before it was cataloged. It would be at Himmler's headquarters if something like that happened."

"Okay, I'll drive wherever you say, I don't mind driving around here, but Dina might get upset if we don't get any results," Jack replied and pressed the gas pedal. Any diversion to the route would also mean more time spent. He would do anything to pass the time just as long as Dina did not get worried and angry and kill them all.

He headed forward, passing the chancellery building.

"The address of the headquarters is number eight Prince Albrecht Street. It's the headquarters of the entire SS," Carl Bosch said.

Jack let his foot off the gas for a moment. It was a scary thought to go directly to the SS headquarters. In any other company, he would have told them to forget it because he was a Brit, and he would certainly be caught and tortured since it was wartime. However, they had Dina in the second car, and she was a demon, a mummy cursed and reborn, and she would protect them.

Jack sighed. Of all the crazy things he had done in his life, this must be the craziest.

41

Himmler

Werner Grothman returned to his office and waited for the five soldiers he had sent to the airport to report back.

In half an hour, *Scharführer* Karl Dorfman called from the airport. He was a seasoned squad leader and had fought in France earlier the same year and then came to work at the headquarters when the position became available. He was a tall man with short wheat-colored hair and wore the symbolically feared black outfit of the SS officers. "We have located the blimp. It's here. It's empty." That was the easiest part of the report. Now came the more difficult part.

"Yes, Excellent news that our airship from Cairo is unharmed. What else did you find there? Where is Helmut?" Werner Grothman replied, leaning back. He sensed something was wrong. No officer usually hesitated when they reported back from their mission.

"We found some skeletons on board the blimp," Karl Dorfman said, and then quickly added, "There was also a pile of skeletons on the ground in front of the airport building. No one was alive. The skeletons had soldiers' outfits. We didn't find any officer uniform on them. Two skeletons were without uniform," Karl reported. He waited for outrage or disbelief, but Werner Grothman was quiet for the longest time before replying. "Thank you. Return to headquarters."

"*Jawohl,* Herr commander," Karl replied and ended the call. Instead of the dreaded fury or blame that they had not done their job, it seemed this was what the headquarters had been afraid they would find there.

Werner Grothman leaned his head on his hands. This was what he had feared. *Helmut Schmidt is dead. He must be the other skeleton with no uniform*, Werner Grothman thought. *He was my friend. They must have taken his uniform to move around the city more freely. The other missing uniform from the soldier must be for the same reason. I must report to Himmler immediately,* he thought and got up, straightened his jacket, brushed his hair back with his hand, and then knocked on Himmler's door.

“Come in,” Himmler called, and Werner Grothman entered and stood still until Himmler was ready to hear what he had to say.

He was writing on his desk, and his forehead was creased as if in deep thought or worried about something. When he finished his work, he signed it, then put it on the right side of the desk on top of a pile of documents already signed. He had been busy going through the state’s affairs and checking out what needed to be done to win the war. Finally, he looked up and leaned back in his chair. He was ready for Werner Grothman’s report.

“The team called back from the airport. I have their report,” Werner Grothman started.

“Go on. What did they find out?” Himmler asked, frowning.

“It seems the whole troop is dead, including the officer we sent there. No one was found alive. They also found skeletons onboard the the airship. Those were most likely our officers onboard when whoever boarded with the supernatural being,” Werner Grothman explained.

Himmler took off his metal-framed glasses and wiped them clean with a large white handkerchief, slowly and meticulously, and put them back on. He looked pensive when he asked, “What do you think happened at the airport?”

“I believe this creature or whatever supernatural being was onboard, attacked our troop and Helmut Schmidt and killed them. They took two uniforms: Helmut’s officer uniform and one of the soldier’s uniforms. I believe they did this because they wanted to find something in Berlin, and with the SS officer’s and soldier’s uniforms, they will be able to find what they are looking for." Werner Grothman took a deep breath and kept his eyes steady.

"Hm, you're probably right. The uniforms were taken because they had a use for them. But what could they be looking for here in Berlin? That's the important question," Himmler said, then asked, "Did they find any Englishmen on board or at the airport? I remember an earlier report that some Englishmen had boarded in Cairo."

Werner Grothman shook his head. "Scharführer Karl Dorfman only found skeletons."

"Ach! So, our German businessmen were not there either?" Himmler asked.

"It is impossible to be sure because all the bodies were skeletons, but I think they are still alive. The skeletons found had German uniforms, and none wore civilian clothes," Werner Grothman replied.

"They asked for an inventory list of what was found in Cairo on tombs. Do you have it?" Himmler asked.

"*Jawohl,* I will go and get it," Werner Grothman replied and exited. He returned soon with a document in his hand and handed it to Himmler, who looked at it. "Nothing special here, but there must be something on it that interests them," Himmler said, reviewing the list. "Sarcophaguses, mummies, pots, pans, small decorative items, and jewelry." Himmler lifted his eyes from the paper and asked, "Was all of it delivered to the warehouse next to the museum?"

"I believe so. Let me double-check," Werner Grothman said and left the room. He went to the list he had gotten from the officer who managed the catalogs of what they received from the different archeological teams. He called him. "I asked you for an inventory list recently received from Cairo. Was there anything else sent from there that was not on the list?"

He waited for the officer to check his lists, listened to his answer, and returned to Himmler's office. "Yes, one item was not with the inventory sent to the warehouse. A golden heart scarab. That was sent to our beloved leader as a gift."

Werner Grothman didn't add that Himmler himself had decided to gift it. Werner Grothman knew that they gifted many valuable artifacts from the collections to their leader such as jewelry and statues directly from the excavations, so it was no surprise that Himmler didn't know what had been in the shipment originally. Some of the items he kept himself, but not this one. He preferred paintings instead of items, even if they were made of gold.

"That's what they are looking for." Himmler slammed his fist on the table. "Now we know what they want. We also know where it is. We must prepare ourselves if we want this supernatural power to be on our side. We must negotiate with it. We have to win it over."

"Where is it now?" Werner Grothman asked curiously.

"All the gifts for our dear Fuhrer were sent to the Berghof for a celebration party that our leader will have to honor our great victory against France," Himmler replied. "All the commanding officers have received the invitation. I will go there. This creature and the others with this demon cannot access this secure home of our leader."

Berghof was Hitler's residence on the same mountain as the Eagle's Nest, where he met the official visitors of the state and high-ranking visitors. Berghof was bought with the money Hitler had earned from his book sales. It was renovated and expanded under Martin Borman's supervision. It was where he went to rest, relax, and celebrate the victories of the war.

42

Himmler Meets Jack and Carl

Werner Grothman paused by the doorway and added, "I got a report from two of our posts in the city. They report seeing two cars with a truck. One of the cars has a skeleton, or rather a mummy, on its roof. I believe this is related to this case."

"Ach, interesting," Himmler mused.

"The patrol said that a woman called out from inside the car and claimed that it was an advertisement for a coming exhibition at the museum," Werner Grothman added.

"It seems the missing passengers and the supernatural being we are looking for are in these vehicles. Do you know where they are going?" Himmler turned his sharp eyes on his assistant and waited for the answer.

"Yes, the last patrol said that they saw the vehicles drive toward the chancellery buildings, and then from there, they turned to head this way," Werner Grothman said.

"Here? Why would they come here?" Himmler rose from his chair behind the desk and walked to the window. He watched the cars pass by and his officers walking out of the headquarters to their vehicles.

"They want to know where the golden artifact is," Werner Grothman replied.

"They already searched the warehouse, and now they come here because they couldn't find what they were looking for there." Himmler nodded to himself and stared outside. "I think our guests have arrived."

Werner Grothman walked to the window and glimpsed outside. "I see. Two of our vehicles and a truck. One vehicle has a mummy on top. Yes, that fits the description I got from the patrol earlier," Werner Grothman commented. "Do you want to arrest them?"

"Let's see," Himmler turned and put his hands behind his back. "They have killed every one of our troops we sent to greet them at the airport, and those are not their only kills, I assume. No, I don't want to go anywhere near them. We need to let them know we can exchange information about the location of the golden scarab if they cooperate with us. Send a man with a note to them and ask a negotiator to come to speak with us."

Werner Grothman paled, but he didn't want to object to SS-Reichsführer Heinrich Himmler because that would mean the end of his career. Instead of complaining about this order, he just raised his right hand and saluted him with his hand extended in front of him, then replied, "*Jawohl*," and exited.

He went to his desk and called the front gate guard. "Stop the three vehicles approaching. SS-Reichsführer Heinrich Himmler wants to talk with them. Approach them carefully. They are lethal," Werner Grothman ordered.

Taking a cigarette from his drawer, he walked to the window to see what happened next in the courtyard. He watched as the guard raised his hand to stop the vehicles. They slowed down and stopped in front of him.

The guard walked slowly to the first vehicle, where Jack was dressed in the officer's outfit. He greeted Jack formally. "SS-Reichsführer Heinrich Himmler wants to speak with you. His assistant asked to stop you and take you upstairs."

"Sure," Jack replied. "What is this all about?"

The guard shook his head. "I only know what I was ordered," the guard replied.

"Let me convey this order to my companion," Jack said, parked the car, and then asked the German businessmen, "Should I go?"

"I can come with you. I've known Himmler for years," Bosch replied, then opened the door and got out. "If he sends an invitation, we better do as he asked. Besides, I'm sure he already knows that his troops at the airport are killed. He wants to know more about this demon we have with us."

Jack went to talk to Sawyer and Lillian. "SS-Reichsführer Heinrich Himmler has asked to talk with us. Do you want me to go with Carl Bosch?"

"We should find out what he wants," Lillian said, and Sawyer nodded. "They might have the golden scarab. You should go. We'll wait here. If we don't see you come out in an hour, then we will come and rescue you… or the mummies will," Lillian replied, looking worried.

"I'll be okay. Bosch thinks Himmler already knows what happened at the airport. This might be a negotiation about the missing artifact," Jack replied. He tapped the hood of Sawyer's vehicle and added, "Wish me good luck." Then he walked to the guard waiting for him with Carl Bosch, and together they followed the guard inside the stone building, which was Himmler's headquarters, more formally known as the Reich Security Main Office.

Inside, the guard led them through the large open hallways with shiny floors and columns to the staircase and jogged up the stairs leading the guests to Himmler's assistant's office. The guard clicked his heels, greeted Werner formally, then turned around with military precision and left the two men with Werner Grothman. He stood there with a half-smoked cigarette in his hand and assessed the men.

Carl Bosch greeted Werner Grothman first, "Good Morning. SS-Reichsführer Heinrich Himmler had asked us to come to meet him here."

Werner glanced at Jack's uniform and frowned. He knew it was Helmut's. Jack saw his glance and replied, "Sorry about the incident at the airport. Our demon killed everyone there. I suspect you knew the officer whose uniform this was."

"Yes, he was my friend," Werner replied stiffly. He stepped out and gestured to the main office where Himmler was. "Let's go inside. SS-Reichsführer Heinrich Himmler is waiting for you. He has an offer for your demon."

"I'm all ears," Jack mumbled and followed Himmler's assistant and Carl Bosch to the next room.

Himmler sat behind his large wooden desk and glanced up when he heard the knock on the door.

Werner stepped inside first, then Carl Bosch, and last, Jack in Helmut's uniform.

Himmler assessed the two men and said slowly, "Herr Bosch, I hope you are in good condition. I've heard many have died who have met this supernatural being traveling with you."

"*Jawohl*, SS-Reichsführer Heinrich Himmler, I am safe if the demon we call Dina gets what he wants. Alfried Krupp, and Friedrich Flick, are also in the car, both of whom you know to be loyal and prominent German businessmen. We had considered that this supernatural being would be a great weapon if we could harness it to serve us," Bosch replied nervously.

"And can it be harnessed?" Himmler interrupted, staring at Carl Bosch with sharp eyes.

"No, I don't believe so." Carl Bosch looked ashamed. "She is very powerful. She can kill with one gesture. She can command mummies to kill."

"Ach," Himmler replied. "Do you know what this demon wants?"

"Yes, she is looking for a golden scarab, a heart stone," Carl Bosch replied. He took out a handkerchief from his pocket and wiped the sweat from his forehead.

"And I know where it was sent," Himmler replied.

Both Carl and Jack looked at him, surprised.

Himmler leaned back, seemingly enjoying the effect of his words. "It's with our dear leader at the Eagle's Nest in an unreachable fortress."

"Ach, but our demon does not know any limits. She can reach anywhere at any time," Carl Bosch replied.

"What will she do with the heart stone?" Himmler asked.

Bosch shook his head and turned to face Jack, who shrugged. "As far as I know, she needs it to stay alive in our world. We believe she has less than forty-eight hours left. If she does not possess that heart stone before the forty-eight hours' end, then I believe she will vanish and return to the underworld, but that's just our assumption," Jack explained.

Himmler stared at his uniform. Jack thought it was best to explain it. "This is not my uniform. I took it from the skeleton at the airport. We thought it would be better to have an officer with our group so we would not have to explain our business here to any patrols. Dina would have caused more chaos and massacre if we had not done so."

Himmler frowned but did not reply.

Werner decided he should say something. "We asked you to come here to negotiate. We know the location of the heart stone, and your demon wants it."

"What kind of a deal do you want to suggest?" Carl Bosch asked, turning to face Himmler.

"We'll give her the golden heart stone in exchange for her powers. She needs to work for us," Himmler replied.

"We can tell her what you want, but I don't know what her answer will be," Carl replied, glancing at Jack, who shook his head almost imperceptibly. Jack knew Dina would not negotiate. She wanted all the power, not to work for anyone else.

"Come back when you have the answer," Himmler ordered and gestured them to leave the room.

Werner closed the door after the two men and asked, "Do you think we can negotiate this demon to work for us?"

"If she wants the heart scarab, we have a chance. With her powers, we will win this war," Himmler replied sternly.

Werner nodded, greeted him officially, and left the room to follow the two men. Jack and Bosch had already gone down the staircase and were halfway through the hallway when he reached them. "Do you believe we can reach a deal?" Werner asked.

"Unofficially or officially?" Jack asked.

"Unofficially," Werner replied quietly.

"No, I don't think demons negotiate at all," Jack said, then walked out the front gate and headed to their vehicles. Carl Bosch followed him, sat next to his business partners, and explained to them what had happened at Himmler's office and his offer.

Meanwhile, Jack walked to the second car, where Dina, Sawyer, and Lillian waited. Jack leaned in through the side window and said, "We got an offer. Himmler knows where the heart stone is. He is willing to get it for you if you work for them. That's his offer."

Lillian translated the offer to Dina, who laughed. "I would never work for anyone in this world if I had the heart stone in my hand. I would be a god on earth."

"That's what I thought," Jack replied. "What do you want to do next?"

"Go get the stone, of course," Dina replied.

"Do you know where it is?" Lillian asked Jack, who nodded. "Do you know a place called the Eagle's Nest?"

Lillian nodded and then paled. "You can't be serious? The heart scarab is with Fuhrer himself?"

Jack nodded and tapped the hood with his hand. "Yes, that's the bad news."

43

Dina's Decision

Dina had sat quietly, watching Jack explain what had happened at the headquarters. She had no idea what the building was or what these soldiers were. She wished they could continue the search. She didn't understand why they had to wait in the car when time was running out.

Lillian turned to her and told her that Jack now knew where the scarab was.

Dina sighed. Finally, some good news. Her eyes lingered on Lillian's face as she said, "Let's go there right now. Why are we still here?"

Lillian broke eye contact and replied, "The leader in this building made an offer. He can get the heart stone for you in exchange for your services on his side of the ongoing war." She did not want to voice her own opinions of what that coalition would do to the world.

Sawyer turned his head, stared at Lillian, and said quietly, "The war would be over if Dina joined the Axis alliance. We cannot let that happen."

When Dina heard the offer, she laughed in a high-pitched voice that sent chills down Lillian's and Sawyer's spines. "I don't need humans to help me get a scarab. I can do it on my own."

Sawyer took a deep breath and said, "That's that, then. Can we go now?" He was relieved. Dina would have changed the course of the war if she had meddled in the battles. He could just imagine an army of living dead mummies attacking allied forces on any front. He shivered. Dina would wipe away whole armies with her force.

Dina leaned forward, tapped Sawyer on the shoulder, and commanded, "Let's leave this place. Go where the scarab is located!"

"Okay, I can do that," Sawyer said and started the car.

Jack saw that Sawyer was leaving and waited until Sawyer's car was next to his, then asked, "What did Dina decide?"

"No alliance and no deal with the Germans. She wants to go to get the scarab herself." Sawyer glanced at the backseat and added, "And she's impatient. She wants to go there right now." He drove ahead, and Jack started his vehicle and drove after Sawyer. The truck with the mummy driver followed them.

Jack stopped by Werner, who was by the front gate, and said, "The demon said no."

Werner nodded. "You were right. Demons don't negotiate. We'll be waiting for you at the Eagle's Nest. You'll never get inside without us."

"Don't be so sure," Jack replied, saluting him casually with his fingers on the brim of his officer's hat. He pressed the gas, and the engine roared as he zoomed forward to catch Sawyer.

Werner stood back, watching them drive away, and walked briskly back inside. He knocked on Himmler's door. "Enter!" he heard Himmler's voice inside, and he opened the door.

Himmler took one look at his face and said, "The demon did not accept our offer. The negotiations are over."

Werner nodded, "That's correct."

"We will send troops to protect the Eagle's Nest. I will make sure our leader is not there when the demon reaches the valley and the mountain area. We can also send a flight battalion to bomb the cars now that we know where they are heading and what vehicles they are driving," Himmler commented and placed his hands on the table in front of him. "We will show the demon that we are more powerful than she thought. She will renegotiate with us."

"*Jawohl,* SS-Reichsführer!" Werner replied and said, "I will go and take care of it now."

After saluting his superior officer formally, he left the room, then walked to his desk, and made a few phone calls. The German's Alpen troops, *Gebirgsjäger,* would be ready, and he also called the Luftwaffe's headquarters and reported to them the situation they had on hand. He described the vehicles the Brits were driving in detail and said they wore SS uniforms, but they were not Germans. He also mentioned that three German businessmen were in the first vehicle and expressed his wish that these men would be spared by the air bombing. He hoped they could save the Germans driving with Jack, but if that was not possible, someone else would have to take over their companies. He knew that the airplane would drop the bombs if they saw the vehicles he had described approaching the Eagle's Nest. There was no doubt in his mind that their first order would be to secure their leader's residence. Too bad if there was some collateral damage.

After making the calls, Werner leaned back and considered what would happen next. He had no idea because they had never faced an enemy like this—a demon.

44

Dina and Sawyer

Both Jack and Sawyer knew that the trip through Berlin would not be easy now that Himmler's headquarters knew who they were and who was with them.

Even Carl Bosch and his colleague Friedrich Flick looked worried in the vehicle's back seat. Friedrich asked quietly from Carl quietly, "Could the driver stop and let us go? We don't have anything to do with the demon. We could go on with our lives without this stress."

Alfried, who sat next to Jack, replied, "Do you think Dina will let us go? I believe we will turn into skeletons in a few seconds. She hasn't said she needs us but has not told us that we are free to go."

Friedrich wiped the sweat from his upper lip and forehead and swallowed loudly. He had not considered that they would need permission to leave from Dina. If he had been alone, he probably would have run out and ended up dead like the soldiers at the airport.

In Sawyer's vehicle, Dina leaned forward and played with Sawyer's hair. "I could offer you a role in my court, but not as a slave." She planted her hand on his shoulder, and Sawyer felt a cold chill and tried hard not to shiver.

"What kind of a role are you talking about?" Sawyer asked, but he didn't want to know what the monster had to offer.

Dina squeezed his shoulder. "You could become my lover. After I possess the heart scarab, I will rule this world and everyone in it. Your position would be to serve me day and night."

Sawyer took a deep breath. What can you say to a demon who wants to rule the world?

Finally, he replied, "It depends on what will happen in this world after you have that scarab in your possession. Will you kill more people, cause an epidemic, or cause the world to end?"

Dina's grip loosened for a moment, and her soft voice turned hard as stone. "Do you believe I'm a monster?"

Sawyer lifted his shoulders. "I don't know you that well. There are so many fairytales where the queen is evil. How do I know you are not one of them?"

Dina's smile faded for a moment, and her eyes turned black. "Are you comparing me to an evil fairytale queen?"

Lillian leaned forward and said quietly, "Sawyer, please. Don't tease her. She is serious." Lillian had been translating this conversation the whole time, and now she saw how Dina's mood had turned from flirtatious to menacing.

Sawyer was in danger.

Dina's expression was dark, and she was not pleased that Sawyer seemed resistant to her charm. Sawyer took the hint and added, "Dina, I don't know you. That's all I'm saying. This is not the time and place to discuss what will happen once you have the scarab in your hands. I'm driving and trying to keep up with Jack and stay on this road. Can we talk about this later?"

Sawyer recoiled inwardly as he turned his head and smiled encouragingly.

Dina batted her eyelashes, surprised: was her suggestion pleasing, or was this a ploy? She wasn't sure. She was not stupid, and she realized that power could be alluring, but also it would put Sawyer in a position to betray her.

Sawyer glanced at her again, gave a more dashing smile, and winked at her. He hoped that would convince the demon that he was interested in her offer.

Dina's eyes narrowed, and she looked suspicious. Dina tapped Sawyer's shoulder lightly and leaned back on the seat. "Yes, we will continue to discuss this later. You are correct: First, the heart scarab, then the fun."

Sawyer nodded, his hand gripping the wheel so tight his knuckles were white. Flirting with Dina was a dangerous game. He could not be sure how Dina would react to rejection. Sawyer chewed his lip in thought. He had to figure out a way to make sure Dina would not get her hands on the scarab; otherwise, his destiny would be grim.

Dina added menacingly, "You should know that no human can kill me. That's not an option. The only one who can take me away from this world is God Anubis. He gave me time to find the scarab; if I get it before the time ends, I can stay and rule in this world."

Sawyer replied, "I know we can't kill you. You have demonstrated it many times." He sighed. "I was serious. I want to take you up on your suggestion later when we have more time. Discussing it here when I need to concentrate on driving is not the best timing. I want to concentrate fully on you, and only you." He hoped he sounded convincing.

Dina's eyes widened, and she smiled like a pleased cat who had gotten a bowl full of cream. "I can't wait," she said in a purring voice.

Sawyer resisted sighing in relief. He viewed Dina from the rearview mirror, and his stomach churned inwardly. Dina looked pleased. Good.

Not much Sawyer could do but obey for now.

If Dina got the scarab, Sawyer knew he would be in trouble. It looked like he was destined to be Dina's lover. The only things standing between that destiny were the hours left of Dina's timeline and the heart scarab.

45

A Drive Through Berlin

The drive through busy daytime Berlin with army vehicles around them was nerve-wracking as they did not know whether Himmler had ordered them to be stopped or to let them proceed through the city. Jack considered both choices and decided that Himmler would likely not start carnage within city limits, but he would easily try to kill them outside in the countryside now that he knew where they were heading. Besides, Himmler could call the Eagle's Nest and ask them to remove the artifact and take it somewhere else, so Jack was not even sure their trip to that remote location was necessary. Then he remembered Dina's timeline and decided any drive would be good because it would use more of Dina's time, and the sooner the demon returned to the underworld, the better.

Sawyer was thinking the same way, except he was more concerned about keeping Dina in the backseat and telling her he was not interested in her. He kept looking in the rearview mirror, and Dina's eyes met his every single time. She winked at him and gave him air kisses.

Sawyer cringed inside. If he could have, he would have stopped the car and run away, but he knew Dina would have sent mummies or the beetles after him, and he would be dead in seconds. The only thing he could think of was to go on and hope that Dina's time ran out.

Dina asked casually, "Is this place far away? I would like to get my reign on earth to start soon."

Lillian glanced at Dina and swallowed hard. *A reign on earth? She wants to rule the whole planet*! "It will take a while to get there."

Dina looked suspicious. "How long?"

Lillian shrugged because she had no idea how far it was. "I don't know. Maybe Sawyer knows." She leaned forward and asked Sawyer, "Do you know how far the Eagle's Nest is? Dina is asking."

Sawyer said, "Many hours. I don't know how good the roads are and if we will be stopped on the way there. I would guess maybe eight hours if the roads are in good condition."

"What should I tell her?" Lillian asked. They both knew Dina would not be happy with the travel time.

"Tell her it will be hours of driving," Sawyer replied.

When Lillian translated that, Dina looked displeased. "Hours? I don't like that. I want the scarab now."

"We can't give you the scarab because it is not here. They had shipped it to the Eagle's Nest. The only thing we can do is to follow it there." Lillian felt Dina's cold black eyes on her.

"How can we get there faster?" Dina asked impatiently.

"There's no way to get there faster. It's a remote location. There's no airport close by, and the only way to get there is to drive," Lillian explained, hoping Dina would accept it.

"I will still have hours after that," Dina muttered.

Lillian looked at Dina and saw that she looked calculating. Dina was correct, though. It had only been one and a half days, so she still had about the same number of hours left. She was not desperate yet. Lillian dared not think what would happen if they failed to reach the Eagle's Nest by late tonight. Dina might be furious and kill them all.

Breathing in and out slowly, Lillian tried to calm herself. She saw Sawyer watching her in the rear-view mirror, and she blinked her eyes once, hoping that Sawyer would understand. They had dodged the fury of the demon for now.

46

The Attack

Jack and Sawyer noted several road patrols on their way out of Berlin, but they seemed to watch them go by instead of ordering them to stop them. They didn't even try to stop their convoy of three vehicles but waved them through.

Suspicious, Jack thought. *It seems that Himmler has other plans for us. How will he try to kill us, or is he planning to capture Dina? Himmler can't be serious if he thinks he can try to renegotiate with Dina. He should realize*

Dina is not a human, and her only wish is to get the scarab. Himmler knows where the scarab is, but I don't see how Himmler could get to the scarab before us, Jack wondered.

Jack looked up and saw two airplanes flying high up with the clouds. He tried to see the symbols on their nose and wings but couldn't.

In the following car, Sawyer saw the airplanes too. He had studied the different models of airplanes because he had smuggled both items and people from Cairo to other places before and after the war had started.

In 1940, the world was divided into two camps: the Nazis and the Axis alliance countries, namely Italy and Japan, which had just signed the pact because Japan wanted to be the prominent power in Asia area, and the Allies, including Great Britain and France because they saw Germany as a threat to their independence and survival. The airplanes' models differed too; by the time Germany had attacked France, the residents had learned how to tell the difference between the Luftwaffe's airplanes from the Allies.

Sawyer knew what Junker's bombers looked like: they had rounder and wider wings than the other models, and when he glanced up, he recognized them. He saw them circling above the road they were driving. He quickly drove off the road next to a forest, hoping the trees would give them some cover. Jack and the mummy vehicle followed his example.

Keeping his engine running, Jack got out of the car and went to talk to Sawyer. "Do you think those are Luftwaffe's planes looking for us?"

"They could be. I know they are Junkers, but I don't know if Himmler sent them to stop us," Sawyer replied. "You better go back to your car because I will leave as soon as those planes are behind the clouds.

"Okay," Jack said and ran back to his car.

Sawyer kept his eyes on the planes, and when they disappeared behind the clouds, he drove back onto the road and pressed the gas. *The further we get from Berlin, the better*, he thought. *Himmler won't know if we are still in the city or outside.*

Meanwhile, Himmler's office had received reports of the three vehicles driving through the city. Each patrol post had called Werner Grothman and reported back; thus, he knew exactly where the vehicles were and their routes. The latest call was from the Luftwaffe informing Werner that two of their bombers had spotted the vehicles just outside Berlin and asked to confirm if SS-Reichsführer Heinrich Himmler would like them to bomb the vehicles.

Werner replied, "Please, hold on. I will ask SS-Reichsführer Heinrich Himmler." He left the phone's handset on the table, stood up, walked to Himmler's door, knocked on it, and waited for his superior to reply. He wanted to double-check that Himmler wanted the bombing because their businessmen were in the first vehicle.

"Enter," Werner heard Himmler's voice from behind the door. He opened it, marched inside, and stopped next to his desk, waiting for Himmler to look up.

"Ja?" Himmler asked, taking off his glasses and rubbing his nose where the glasses had pressed red marks on both sides. He had dark circles under his eyes because neither he nor his assistant had slept for over twenty-four hours. A long sleepless night and the stress of a demon on the loose had kept them both alert and awake.

"The convoy has been located outside the city limits. Do you wish the bombers to drop bombs? It will kill the German businessmen too?" Werner asked.

Himmler considered the choices for a moment, then said, "Our bomber pilots are very accurate. I'm sure they can aim at the two last vehicles and save our citizens. However, if they miss, then that's war." He shrugged and turned his eyes back to the paperwork on his desk.

Werner greeted him and left the office. Outside, he sat by his desk, grabbed his phone's handset again, and said, "Ja, SS-Reichsführer Heinrich Himmler wants your bombers to drop the bombs. Try to avoid the first vehicle, but if that is not possible, they will be casualties of war." He listened to the reply and hung up.

He sat there quietly, wondering what would happen if the bombs hit the first vehicle. Who would run the German companies if their prominent leaders were killed today? He knew well that they needed Carl Bosch to fund the war efforts, and his company was also part of the group concentrating on chemical warfare. Alfried Krupp of Krupp Group produced artillery, ammunition, battleships, U-boats, and tanks. And the third one, Friedrich Flick of Flick companies, assisted in war efforts and had just started using war criminals as workers in their coal mines to reduce costs in their industry. If the worst happened, and the business leaders were killed, the companies would have to regroup and find a way to continue because

Werner knew they needed the big companies in this war. They could not do without them and their support.

When the Luftwaffe's pilots had gotten the word to bomb, they returned to the same area where they had spotted the vehicles. They saw them driving along the same road further away. They zoomed downward and dropped two bombs each. They saw the direct hit on the truck, and then two bombs hit the road next to the vehicles, and one hit in between the two vehicles. The smoke billowed high up in the air, and it was hard to see if they had succeeded in destroying the second vehicle. They flew over and saw all three vehicles stopped on the road. All looked damaged by the bombs, and they did not see any movement near the vehicles. The road now had two deep holes where the bombs had exploded and a mess of metal from the truck. The first car looked as if the explosion had hit the back of the car, and the second vehicle had a mangled front.

The bomber pilots reported back to their headquarters that their mission was successful. Werner received the call from Luftwaffe's headquarters, which he then forwarded to Himmler.

Himmler looked suspicious. "They said they bombed the cars and saw no movement?"

"That is correct, sir," Werner replied.

Himmler shook his head. "I don't believe it. The demon and her mummies would have come out. You can't kill them with bombs. I believe they killed the humans in the cars but not the demon."

"What do you want me to do?" Werner asked.

"Ask a fighter jet to fly by and see if there is any movement on the road either by the bomb site or otherwise. I believe our demon has escaped." Himmler gestured with his hand that the conversation was over and Werner was allowed to leave.

When Werner returned to his desk, he called Luftwaffe's headquarters, informed them of Himmler's request, and waited for them to call back. He sat back on his chair and wondered where the passengers went if they were not in the vehicles. The bomber pilots had said the cars were moving on the road. Were the vehicles empty?

47

What Happened?

Jack recalled the newspaper articles that had praised Germany as a newborn country back in 1930 before Hitler had started the war. If only they had known what would happen ten years later. He also remembered how they had described Himmler as a workaholic and a cunning strategist. He was also the most powerful officer after Hitler and had shaped the SS's development into a powerful war machine. *We'll see how cunning he is*, Jack thought.

When Jack realized Junkers were following the cars, he waited until the planes were among clouds, then quickly stopped by the roadside, and Sawyer and the truck followed his example. Jack had an idea: Let the mummies drive the vehicles and see if the planes returned to bomb them. He explained to Lillian, who translated the request to Dina, who approved it. They stayed behind while the mummies continued driving.

Jack wasn't sure if Himmler planned to do that, but they would know for sure this way. He suspected Himmler would try to stop them before the Eagle's Nest, so the road with few tanks and cars would be a perfect opportunity.

"We can't wait here," Jack said. "Let's start walking. We'll find some other transportation soon, I hope."

Dina stopped. "I'm not walking with this narrow skirt and these ridiculous pointy-heeled shoes"." She turned to the rest of the mummies—only three went with the vehicles—and ordered, "Carry us to our destination. Fast!" The first mummy grabbed her in its bony arms, and the next ones took Lillian and Sawyer. Dina latched her black eyes on Jack and said, "You have proven to be useful... sometimes. You can come with us too." The next mummy picked him up in its arms. Then Dina turned to face the Germans and said, "I'll let you go. I don't need your services. You did your best to help me, but it was not good enough."

The German businessmen paled, as they were not sure what she had said. Bosch quickly looked at Lillian and asked, "Is she going to kill us here?"

Lillian said to Dina, "We are in a hurry. Leave these men behind."

Dina considered this request for a moment and nodded. She ordered the mummies, "Let us go now." The mummies rushed ahead with Dina and the others in their arms, leaving behind the businessmen. They looked relieved.

At that moment, the bombers returned and bombed the vehicles on the road. The blast of the bombing hit the businessmen and threw them to the ground, whereas Dina and her collaborators were already further away. Jack turned in the mummy's arm and looked behind his shoulder. The vehicles were now destroyed, and only smoke and flames were in their place. The road had deep holes where the bombs had hit. His plan had succeeded, but for how long.

Jack saw Junkers flying lower as they checked the site for survivors. He knew the pilots would not see anyone at the crash site. When they report that to Himmler, he won't believe the hit was successful...unless the pilots saw the German businessmen. He glanced back and saw Carl Bosch stumble back on the road. He had a head wound and was bleeding. His clothes were tattered.

He waved his hands to get the attention of the pilots. One of Junkers flew closer and then reported back to Berlin that the prominent business-man seemed to have survived and asked to send a car to pick him up. They didn't see the other businessmen because Alfried and Friedrich Flick were both unconscious by the roadside where the blast had thrown them.

Werner Grothman answered the phone at Himmler's office and listened to what Luftwaffe reported to him. He quickly went back to Himmler and said, "Herr Reichsführer, Carl Bosh has been seen at the site of the bombing alive. Do you want him to be brought here to be interrogated?"

"Yes, of course," Himmler replied.

Werner left his office, went back to the phone, and told the order to bring Carl and any other survivor back to SS Headquarters.

It took half an hour before three businessmen were back at the SS Headquarters where they had been earlier the same day. Now, they looked more like victims than wealthy manufacturers.

At first, Himmler did not believe that the mummies carried the others away, but when all three men swore it had happened, he had to accept that fact. The only question was now, how far did they go with the mummies? How fast could the mummies run? He had no idea.

It was obvious that the businessmen had not successfully convinced Dina to the German side of the war, although they all said they had tried to do that since the blimp. That was a disappointment to Himmler as he had wished to have a demon on their side. "With her supernatural powers, Germany could easily win the war," Himmler said and slapped his palm on the desk in front of him.

Alfried shook his head, "No, I don't think this Dina wants to be on anyone's side. She's on her own. She is too powerful to control."

"That could be," Himmler replied. "We don't want her to be on the Allied side either. It would be better if she was destroyed if she didn't join us. We don't want anyone else to compete with us on leading this world."

"She will return to the underworld if she does not get her scarab," Carl commented. "We might not have to do anything if she fails."

Himmler stared at him. “We will watch the situation and follow them. Thutmose’s Scarab is safe at the Eagle’s Nest.”

“For now,” Carl mumbled.

“For now,” Himmler repeated. He stared at the men in front of him and asked, “You have all visited the Eagle’s Nest. Do you believe someone can enter that place without our soldiers capturing or killing him?”

Carl looked at his colleagues, and they all shook their heads. “That would be true if you spoke of humans, but Dina is a demon or something like that. She can do things we can’t even comprehend. It is possible for her to enter that residence.”

Himmler tapped the tabletop in front of him with a pen and replied, “Then we must make sure our leader will not be there when Dina arrives. Also, we must keep the scarab away from her for…” He frowned and asked, “How many hours do you think she has left?”

“Maybe thirty hours or less,” Carl said. “I remember Anubis told Dina that one day was gone and two left. Now, two days are almost gone, so one more to go.”

Himmler leaned back. “Good, we’ll keep Dina and her collaborators busy, and Dina will disappear after her time is gone.”

“Let’s hope she does that,” Alfried muttered to himself.

Himmler glanced at him, then said, “You can go now. The state will not hold you responsible for anything that has happened.” He nodded to Werner Grothman, who escorted the men out of his office.

All three men glanced at each other and took deep breaths. “I hope it’s over. I don’t want to meet Dina again,” Carl commented.

Werner gestured to the stairway and said, "I'm sure you'll be pleased to go home now. I will arrange a car to take you."

"Thank you," Carl replied, and the others followed him to the stairs and out of the headquarters.

"Is it over?" Alfried asked quietly as they descended the large staircase to the hallway.

"I'm glad that SS-Reichsführer Himmler did not hold us responsible for anything that Dina and the Brits did," Carl remarked and glanced back to make sure no one heard his comment. "Dina is a monster. I hope she will return to where she came from." They walked fast through the hallway, and the soldiers at the front door opened the door for them and stepped outside. A car was waiting for them. They looked at each other: *is it safe to go into that car? Will it take us to our homes or to a prison to be interrogated?*

The driver was also an SS officer. When he noticed the hesitation, he said, "I have orders to take you home." He opened the door, and the three business tycoons sat inside.

48

The Mummy Ride

The mummies were much faster than normal human walking. They were supernaturally fast. In only four hours, they reached the woods surrounding the Berchtesgaden, the Eagle's Nest (Kehlsteinhaus)—a secluded building on top of Mount Kehlstein. The party had given it to Fuhrer as a gift for his fiftieth birthday. It was Hitler's Southern Headquarters and also where the high officials and other prominent visitors would gather to meet the Fuhrer and the other high-ranking members of the Nazi party.

Jack had learned from Himmler that the scarab was sent as a gift to Hitler's summer resort, which was a small cabin on the side of the mountain, not the Eagle's Nest, but he could not be sure if Hitler had taken the heart stone from his residence to the Eagle's Nest.

The scarab could be anywhere by now, Jack mused. *Hitler didn't have to keep the stone for himself. He could have gifted it to Mussolini or someone else in his closest circle. Who knows?*

"Let's stop here," Jack suggested when they reached the edge of the woods. It was safer to stay in the cover of the trees in case the bombers returned. They would not see them through the thick spruce and pine branches.

Lillian translated Jack's suggestion, and Dina ordered the mummies to stop and let them down. Jack never understood how the mummies knew where to go. He had never given an exact location where they were to go, so how did they know the landmarks without anyone telling them? He scratched his head. Perhaps, the creatures from the underworld knew more of the living world than humans realized.

However, while Jack, Sawyer, and Lillian surveyed the area and the distant mountain and kept an eye on the soldier patrols in the woods, they tried to figure out how to best get in. They didn't go near the village because they were sure someone would notice them and report back to Himmler.

It is good it isn't winter and snowy yet, Jack thought. *The patrols would see our footprints too easily in the snow.*

At the bottom of the mountain, Jack saw a large parking area built for visitors and several patrols guarding the entrance to the elevator tunnel. He watched as a car approached. The visitor wore a German uniform, but he was not anyone Jack recognized. The car slowed down, and the patrol checked his credentials and the invitation to the mountain resort. Then the car moved slowly to the tunnel to drop off the visitor, and after a few moments passed, the car returned.

Jack guessed the elevator inside the mountain took the guest up to the top of the mountain. *It will not be easy to get in*, he thought.

Jack noticed the changing of the guards happening at five p.m. He did not know if this happened every six or eight hours or even longer. It could be shorter, too, Jack pondered, because this was where the top officials met.

The visitor was only inside for a short time and then returned to the parking lot.

What Jack and the others did not know was that Himmler had ordered the German Alpen troops, *Gebirgsjäger,* to help secure the mountain against the Brits and Dina. They patrolled along the mountainside and used their binoculars to see all the movements down the hill and approaching the mountain.

Jack turned to Lillian and asked, "We know the scarab was sent as a gift to Fuhrer, but we don't know if it is still at his residence or on top of the mountain at the Eagle's Nest. It could be in either one."

Lillian nodded and explained what Jack had said to Dina. "We go first to the smaller building and then to the next," Dina replied haughtily. She stood ahead of her mummies, which hovered near her waiting for her next command. She had ten mummies with her. Only four had carried them here. One of them was the high priest, Thutmose, who also was Dina's father.

Jack's eyes moved from one mummy to the next. He could not recognize which one was the father-mummy. He turned to Lillian and asked, "Could Dina's father find out where the scarab is and grab it? Do we have to risk our lives trying to get in when she has all the mummies available?"

Lillian nodded and translated the question to Dina.

After she heard what Jack asked, Dina looked around to find his father's mummy, and when she recognized him, she took him aside and they conversed about something. Then Dina turned her back on the mummy, walked back, and replied to Lillian and Jack, "I can send my father to find it, but he will not be able to touch the scarab. It was his, but because God Anubis made his scarab the token for eternal life and dominance on earth, my father cannot take it or remove it. He can point to where it is, but nothing else."

"I should have known that," Jack mumbled.

Sawyer tried to stay away from Dina, being afraid of her affectionate moments like one in the car. Now, he took a couple of steps closer to Jack and said, "If Dina's father can find out where the scarab is, then it will be easier for us to come up with a plan to get it."

Dina watched Sawyer talking and then approached with a honeyed smile. “My darling.” She stood close to him, rested her hand on his back, and gently moved it up and down.

Sawyer swallowed hard. He wanted to shrug, but instead, he forced himself to stand still. Dina’s hand moved upward to caress his neck and twirl his hair between her fingers.

Jack saw Sawyer’s dilemma, and the corner of his mouth quirked up. He quickly turned his face away from Dina and Sawyer so that Dina would not notice.

Lillian moved next to Jack and asked, “If we find that the scarab is in one of the buildings, how do we get it?”

Jack faced Lillian and said with a solemn voice. “I don’t know yet. I think we have to proceed one step at a time. First, find out if the heart stone is in either one of the buildings. If it is, then we can figure out how to get it. If it’s not, then we are in trouble.”

Lillian nodded. “Yes, you are right. We can’t make plans if we don’t know where it is or who has it now.”

They faced Sawyer and Dina again. Lillian said, “Could you send your father to check out the buildings? If he senses the heart scarab, then he can tell where it is.”

Dina nodded. She gestured to her father-mummy, who came closer. Dina gave a quick, sharp order to the father-mummy, who bowed his head and ran away as fast as a leopard. Their eyes followed the mummy as he reached the parking lot. A guard noticed the mummy and tried to shoot him, but he ripped him apart. The next soldier aimed a shot at the mummy, but his shot only penetrated his mummy wraps and could not stop him. The mummy leaped on the soldier like a lion on prey, tearing his head off, and tossed it on the ground. Next, the mummy jumped on the mountainside and started climbing upwards.

The Alpen troops noticed a strange movement on the mountainside and tried to get a better view of what or who it was. "It looks like a mummy. Could this be the attack Himmler's office warned us?" one of the soldiers asked, and the officer in charge took the binoculars and pointed them to the mountainside. He saw the wrapped figure climbing up at a superhuman speed. "Yes, I think that's the threat he warned us about," the officer agreed. "Shoot him."

The soldiers aimed at the mummy and fired. The shots peppered the mountainside on both sides of the mummy, and some hit him, but they did not stop his climb.

"Throw a grenade at the creature!" the officer ordered.

The soldier next to the officer obeyed the command and aimed at the climbing mummy. The grenade exploded in the air above the mummy, who was still below Berghof and the Eagle's Nest. The explosion made the mummy lose his grip, and he fell. However, as he was already dead, it did not cause him any damage. He got up and brushed his tattered wraps, then started climbing back.

"The explosion made him fall, but he's back climbing," the soldier replied. "He is not dead."

"We need to go down to the resort and protect it against this monster," the officer replied, and the troops moved fast downwards. They reached the Berghof in record time, and so did the mummy.

The troops stood in front of the building, rifles aimed at the mummy.

The mummy stopped, opened his mouth wide, and growled at them, showing his mouth with some teeth missing. The soldier took a step back. This was not a normal enemy soldier. The mummy held out hands, grabbed the first soldiers' rifles, pulled them away, and threw the men down the mountain. Their terrified screams echoed until they suddenly stopped. Some soldiers tried to shoot him, but he only staggered with the hits and did not stop. The mummy jumped on the rest of the soldiers and ripped their heads and arms off, creating bloody carnage. The officer stood in front of the door. He was the last one alive. The mummy faced him and grabbed him by the neck. The officer struggled and tried to get the bony fingers off his throat, but they strangled him to death. Now, the mummy was free to go inside.

The resort was empty. The mummy sniffed around but did not sense the scarab there. He walked out and continued to the next target, the building on top of the mountain.

Jack craned his neck to see the mummy and the carnage better. Then he asked Lillian and Sawyer, "Do you think Hitler is there?"

Sawyer shook his head. "No, he's not. Himmler has warned him to stay away."

“That explains why the visitor left so suddenly. They probably knew we were coming and emptied the buildings. They didn’t want any high-ranking officers or visitors to die today,” Jack replied.

And the same carnage happened in the next building.

This time the mummy sensed the scarab’s presence. He had fulfilled Dina’s order, and it was time for him to return to her. He leaped out, descended the mountainside, and ran to the forest to report his finding to Dina.

49

Anubis Returns

When the Thutmose mummy returned to Dina and reported back, she knew she was close to winning the game because it was between her and Anubis, between her survival or returning to the underworld.

Dina looked ravishing with her black eyes shining as she turned to Jack and Lillian and commanded, "We know the scarab is in the building on the top of the mountain. My father confirmed it. It's time for you slaves to show your worth and get it for me."

Jack glimpsed at the mountain and the building high up on top of the mountain and shook his head. "How do you think we can get there? There are still guards at the bottom of the mountain. We saw that they have the changing of guards, so that will happen sometime. The guards that were at the parking area are killed, but I bet if they don't report to their superiors regularly, someone will come and check out what's going on. We will see more troops coming this way. This is the most secure and guarded place in the whole area. Besides, it's not certain we can go up there, find the scarab, and return here alive."

Dina gestured with her hand, and Jack felt an invisible hand strangling him by the throat. "Slave, do you want to die here and now, or do you want to go and get me the scarab?"

Lillian had paled and rushed to help Jack. "Of course, we will help to get it. Jack is only considering the best way to go there, aren't you, Jack?"

Jack tried to nod while the invisible hands grasped his throat. He could not say a word, and his face turned dark red.

Dina lowered her hand, and the strangling sensation ended.

Jack coughed and fell to his knees. He breathed heavily for several minutes. Then he rose back up and said with a quiet voice, "I was going to add that we will need your mummies' help to get there. We don't have guns or ammunition. If someone shoots us, we will bleed and die. That's not going to help you. We need your mummies as guards to go first and clear the path for us so we can get to the elevator and take it to the top."

Sawyer said, "Yes, that would make sense. And I will go with Jack and Lillian." When Dina turned her black eyes on him and frowned, Sawyer added, "Three persons will find it faster than two. Your mummies can't help them find or touch the scarab, so we must do it."

The shadows grew darker around them. It was late in the evening, but it had not been so dark earlier.

Dina looked around first curiously, then in fear. Her face turned ashen, and she leaned against the trunk of a thick pine tree and shivered.

Lillian and Jack noticed the sudden change in her demeanor and quickly scanned the area. They did not find anything suspicious or threatening.

"What's going on?" Jack whispered to Lillian.

"I don't know. She seems to feel something is coming: a threat to her or us. I don't know. She is not threatening us now. She's afraid."

Sawyer positioned himself so that his back was against Jack and Lillian. He looked up, making sure nothing was coming above them while they slowly moved under a taller spruce tree whose trunk would give them more protection if someone attacked them. They kept looking around, but they didn't see anyone moving. The only change was the darkness which seemed to creep closer and engulf the area around them.

One longer shadow formed in front of Dina, changing to a head of a jackal.

"Anubis!" Lillian whispered.

"Dina!" Anubis growled, showing his big jackal teeth. He grew bigger and taller than Dina and loomed over her, ignoring the humans and concentrating on Dina.

"I still have time," Dina said with an unsteady voice.

"Two days are gone, one left," Anubis warned with a menacing growl.

"I know where the scarab is. I can get it," Dina assured.

"You will not use the mummies. On the last day among the living, you will be mortal like the humans. You will not have the help of the underworld," Anubis said, and when he said that, the mummies withdrew to the shadows and disappeared on earth. Dina shivered, and she looked smaller and weaker.

"You can't do this! We had a deal!" Dina argued.

"Gods don't make deals. You either find the scarab on your own, or you die trying. That's the only deal you will get," Anubis replied and disappeared back into the shadows. The darkness faded as the god of the underworld vanished from the earth.

Dina breathed heavily. When she lifted her eyes, they were no longer black but dark brown like human eyes. She looked at her hands and tried to gesture to command the shadows, but nothing happened. She tried again, then cried out in anger. She had lost her skills to control the mummies.

But when she called out the black beetles, they came. She had not lost all the skills. She gestured to Jack, and the invisible hands started to choke him. The only thing she had lost was the help of the underworld, and the dead mummies had returned to their rightful place.

Lillian went to Dina and said, "Stop strangling Jack. We need him. I won't go anywhere if you kill him."

Dina lowered her hand, and Jack was free again. He choked and fell to his knees on the ground. "She still has some power over us. She is not like humans even if Anubis said so," Sawyer commented quietly to Lillian, hoping that Dina did not hear him.

Lillian whispered back, "She is mortal now. She can be killed."

"Good," Sawyer hissed back. "I'm tired of her threats and innuendos."

50

THE NEW PLAN

"I can't believe this! I was promised revenge and eternal life when I returned!" Dina marched around, fuming. "This is cheating! I had a chance when I had control of my mummies. Now, what do I have?" She glared at the others like we were less than mosquitos she would like to swat away. "I have humans!"

Dina stomped her feet. "I want my mummies back!"

She is acting like a spoiled child, Lillian thought. *Perhaps she is that. Her life was cut off when she was a young woman. She did not have time to live and learn the way any normal person did. Also, her life was protected by living with a high priest. I bet she didn't have many chances to disobey and do what she wanted.*

Lillian winced. She should not feel sorry for Dina. She was a monster who should not be alive today. She should return to the underworld where she belonged.

After raging for a while, Dina calmed down. She looked at us and commanded, "I need the scarab. Go get it."

Lillian translated Dina's order, but Sawyer took a step forward and placed himself between Dina and the other two. "You need to come with us. We know where the scarab is, but we don't know what it looks like. What if there are several heart stones in that building? How would we recognize the right one? You are the only one who knows."

That was a sound point. Even if Dina wanted to stay safe and let the others go to danger, she had to admit that Sawyer's words made sense.

Dina opened her mouth and then closed it. She could not find any argument against what Sawyer had said. Finally, she sighed and replied with a defeated voice, "I will go with you." She pushed her fingers through her hair. "How do we do this?"

Sawyer turned to face the others and asked, "Any ideas?"

Jack sat on the ground, rubbing his throat, which Dina had strangled just minutes ago. He could still feel the tight grip of the invisible fingers pressing the life out of him. He didn't want to do anything to help her, but he knew that they had to suggest something. Any idea would show Dina that they were still trying to help her. So, after reasoning all that, Jack said, "I have an idea."

Everyone's eyes went to Jack. He cleared his throat. "We should go to the village. The food is delivered to the Eagle's Nest from there. I don't know who makes it or delivers it, but if we get our hands on the delivery truck, we can pretend to be the employees delivering the food."

Lillian raised her eyebrows. "That idea is pretty good."

She looked at Sawyer, who nodded. "Yes, that could work."

Dina waited and tapped her foot, irritated and impatient. Lillian faced Dina and explained the new plan.

Dina's face brightened, and she agreed. "It will work." She took off her high-heeled shoes and walked barefoot. She gestured for the others to follow her, and they marched down the hill toward the nearest village. They had seen it when the mummies carried them to the woods. Taking advantage of the evening dusk, we walked down the hill. We saw the village's lights below us.

Berchtesgaden in Bavaria was not a large sprawling village. The Nazis had renovated a hotel for important guests and built a railway there. They had done that because the Fuhrer enjoyed that area so much, so they needed to accommodate other visitors coming to that area to meet him.

51

The Nazis

The walk through the woods was peaceful. Sawyer hoped that Dina would leave him alone, but she kept eyeing him and commenting, "Sawyer, you are so strong. You could probably carry me down the hill," and "Sawyer, your powerful arms would help me to go down this road." Tilting her head, Dina looked pleadingly at Sawyer, who went ahead without any reply, even though Lillian dutifully translated all of Dina's loving requests.

Dina looked grumpy, and Lillian was about to warn Sawyer not to upset her, when Jack pointed out, "Look! Soldiers coming up the hill. We need to hide."

They quickly surveyed the road ahead and then the woods behind them. There was no good place to hide. They went behind the nearest trunks and bushes, hoping the soldiers would not notice them. Jack and Lillian lay flat on the ground watching the patrol of twenty men with an officer leading it. Their hopes soon disappeared as the leading officer saw some movement in the forest and called the next two soldiers to go and check it out.

"We're caught!" Jack whispered to Lillian. They were both on the ground, trying to be as flat as possible. "Is it better to surrender now?"

"I don't know," Lillian whispered back. She kept her eyes on the soldiers.

They had caught a glimpse of Dina standing behind a trunk. She wasn't even looking at the soldiers but was fussing about her skirt, which had needles and dried leaves on it.

The soldiers ordered: "Halt!"

Dina didn't care. She heard someone yelling but didn't understand the meaning of the word. She bent down and frowned as she saw the condition of her feet after walking barefoot. She had her high-heeled shoes in one hand, and she leaned on the trunk, her back toward the soldiers.

When Sawyer noticed that Dina wasn't listening to the orders. He lifted his arms and said, "We surrender." He thought that was a better choice than letting Dina the demon conquer the world.

Dina heard his voice and her eyes sparkled. She believed Sawyer had done that because he was infatuated with her. She smiled and took a couple of steps toward him when the soldiers came close and yelled again to stop moving: "*Halt*!"

Frowning, Dina turned and glared at the men who disturbed her. She lifted her hand, gestured to the soldiers, and said, "Go, my little pets. Do your duty." The beetles scurried out of her sleeves and under her skirt as if she was made of black scarab beetles.

The soldiers had no idea what to think when they saw swarming black beetles coming out of the woman and scurrying toward them. They stood there, rifles pointing to the woman and the man, and watched as the beetles reached them. Any escape attempt would have been futile. These were not normal bugs but supernatural creatures from the world of the dead.

The beetles reached the two soldiers, who stared first puzzled and next horrified as the bugs buried inside their clothes and dug through their skin. They cried in terror, asking someone to help them, "*Hilfe*!" When the beetles ate through their organs, they collapsed on the ground, twisting and crying until they stopped moving. Their death was horrible, and they died in agony. When the beetles had done their deed, they returned to Dina.

Sawyer, Lillian, and Jack had seen the beetles and what they could do, so they were not surprised, although Lillian did not want to watch. She quickly turned her head and covered her ears. She didn't want to see or hear the desperate cries.

The other soldiers in the patrol did not believe their eyes. Their comrades had died in front of their eyes, most peculiarly. Black scarab beetles did not exist in the Bavarian Alps. What they saw could not have been real.

But it was real. The two soldiers were dead. The officer in charge shouted, "Shoot them! Shoot them to death!"

The remaining soldiers quickly kneeled, took their rifles, and peppered the forest around Sawyer, Lillian, Jack, and Dina.

Sawyer pulled Dina down without even thinking. He acted on instinct to protect a person under fire. Dina fell to the ground next to him. After, Sawyer realized he should have left Dina where she was. The soldiers could have killed her. Cursing inwardly, Sawyer blamed himself for being stupid and tired of all this.

It is time to stop this, Jack thought. He pulled out a large white handkerchief from his pocket and waved at it. "We surrender!"

The firing stopped.

Jack glanced behind the trunk and saw that the officer had raised his arm, and the soldiers were still in a shooting position, rifles ready if the officer gave the order. "Come out!" the officer called.

Jack slowly got up and raised his arms high up in the air holding the white handkerchief in his right hand and moving to where the officer could see him.

"Come this way!" the officer ordered.

Jack nodded to Sawyer, Dina, and Lillian, and they followed her and walked in the direction of the road where the patrol was.

When they came closer, the officer turned to his men and ordered, "Capture them. These must be the spies we were warned about. They have our uniforms, but they are not Germans. Now, they will be our prisoners."

The soldiers ran to the small group and surrounded them.

Jack and Sawyer handed their Walther P-38s to the arresting soldiers. They had not even used their pistols. Why would they? Dina was all the firepower they needed.

When Jack, Sawyer, Lillian, and Dina were checked to make sure they carried no more weapons, the soldiers poked them with their rifles to move forward.

As they approached the patrol, Sawyer observed that the officer was a *Schutzstaffel* officer, probably sent by Himmler to find them. Yet the soldiers were likely part of German's Alpen troops, *Gebirgsjäger*, although he had never seen them, since they were now in the Alps. They knew the area and the mountains the best and they would not send just any soldier to protect Fuhrer.

Dina growled fiercely, or that's what Sawyer thought she did because the sound was more like an animal's growl than any sound a human would make. He whispered to Lillian, "Tell Dina to relax. This patrol might have done us a favor. They might take us where we want to go." Lillian moved closer to Dina and whispered quickly what Sawyer had said. Dina calmed down, glimpsed at Sawyer, and almost smiled.

However, Sawyer had no idea if that was true. The only thing he wanted was to spend more time. The more time passed, the less likely it was for Dina to get her hands on the heart stone. That was all that mattered. He realized that he was in enemy territory and the SS soldiers were famous for their rude and vicious interrogation methods. He would have been scared to death in any other situation except now when he had to choose between the SS soldiers or the demon. He was not sure which choice was worse, but one thing was sure, none of their options were good.

The officer ordered four men to pick up the dead soldiers from the woods and bring them with them.

The soldiers marched them down the hill where they had parked their trucks and then pointed at one of the trucks, and ordered, "Climb inside." When they had climbed in, the soldiers followed them and sat on both sides. Their faces were solemn. The two closest ones to the prisoners were young and skinny and they looked alike as if they were brothers. They were round-faced, and they had peach fuzz under their nose as if they had tried to grow mustaches.

Lillian heard the two soldiers whispering, "Do you think what we saw was real?"

She glimpsed at them. She realized this was the first time they had witnessed a supernatural thing happening. She knew what would happen when the beetles ran out of Dina. She was prepared but these young men were not.

The other one of the soldiers replied, "It was a hallucination. I don't believe it happened."

The two dead soldiers, or what was left of them, mostly bones and clothes, and some pieces of skin and muscle hanging on the bodies were carried to the last truck.

The two brothers watched the bodies being carried to the last truck.

"That's not a hallucination. They are dead," the other one commented quietly. His face was pale as he watched a skeleton's hand hanging down and only some strings of joints and muscles kept the skeleton together.

"Then what happened? I don't believe a swarm of beetles appears like that. It's not natural!" the other brother replied. He pushed his soldier's helmet back on his head and scratched his skin.

Sawyer said, "Believe me, it happened." He watched as the two brother soldiers looked at each other and then shook their heads.

Both the soldier brothers turned their eyes on him, and Sawyer added, "You saw beetles because there were beetles. Where they come from, I have no idea. They just appear when Dina wants them to kill. I have seen it happen a couple of times. The first time I didn't believe my eyes either, but now I'm used to it." He leaned back on the hard seat on the side of the truck and watched as the soldiers turned their eyes from him to Dina and back. They shook their heads in disbelief.

"You don't have to believe me." Sawyer shrugged and put his hands behind his head. "You can try to explain what happened in the woods any way you like but there is no other explanation than what you saw. It happened."

The two soldiers laughed. The first one replied, "This is some kind of a magic trick. You killed two of our comrades with some weapon. There is no supernatural way to kill people like you try to convince us."

At that moment, the same officer came to check on the truck and the prisoners. He had heard the soldiers talking with Sawyer when he approached the vehicle, so he ordered, "Don't talk with the prisoners. Reichsführer of the Schutzstaffel, Himmler, has ordered to find and capture them, and we will take them to our prison."

Jack sighed. He had to admit Sawyer had been correct in his assumption. These soldiers acted on behalf of Himmler, and they would take us to the mountain camp or even up to the top where the scarab was. Then Jack frowned as he questioned in his mind, *why would Himmler want us captured? Himmler knew we were after the scarab, and he told us where it was.* Then Jack realized, *that Himmler does not know about Anubis's last visit. He does not know that Dina can be killed.*

The soldiers would have killed all of us in the woods if they had thought that would be possible. The soldiers were not told that they were after a demon, Jack thought. *They were ordered to capture a group that was threatening the Third Reich. Himmler wanted Dina to be on German's side. He had told us that much. He didn't believe we would be here this soon. However, now that we are captured, does Himmler have a new offer for Dina? Would it include us at all?*

And Jack was correct: Himmler wanted to show Dina how powerful German was and what she could gain by allying with them. Himmler also knew that Dina was running out of time. The German businessmen had told him that Dina would be on Earth only for a certain number of hours, and they had told him what the Anubis had said in the warehouse: "One day is gone, two left."

And now another day had gone. It was already late in the evening. Less than one day left to find the heart stone, Jack thought. *Maybe this world will survive Dina, or maybe not. We'll see...*

The trucks' engines started with a roar and the vehicles jerked to start. They were on their way to a German prison, Jack thought.

52

THE DRIVE

The trip went up the hill and not toward the village below.

Jack and Sawyer glanced at each other. Sawyer asked the soldiers, “Where do you take us?”

The soldiers glanced at each other and then the other one of the brothers leaned to check on the front where the officer sat to make sure he didn’t hear them, and then he replied with a quiet voice, “We were ordered to find a group of enemy spies. I guess they are you although you don’t look like spies." Two women and two men in normal clothing who had no weapons or fighting skills... except the weird magic trick they had used in the forest. The soldier had not seen or heard any weapons fired, and they didn't believe their comrades were dead. How could they die without any explosion or shots fired? Whatever these prisoners possessed was a powerful weapon, the soldier thought. "Reichsführer Himmler ordered us to take you to the prison."

"Where is the prison?" Sawyer asked. He had heard what the officer had said, but he wanted to know the exact location of their prison.

The soldier replied, "It's below the Eagle's Nest at the bottom of the mountain. We have a camp there because we protect the important visitors to the Eagle's Nest and Berghof."

"Ah, thank you," Sawyer replied and leaned back and closed his eyes. *What a mess. Any smuggling trip would have been better than this. I'm in the truck with SS soldiers on my way to prison. What did I do that day in Cairo when I let myself be found in a bar in Hotel Alhambra? I should not be drinking that much. I used all the money I had earned from the smuggling to drink,* Sawyer thought, feeling sorry for himself. He still had the soldier's uniform on, but the holster was empty. He brushed a strand of brown hair that hung on his forehead back.

Jack leaned closer to Sawyer and muttered to him in English, "Why did you save her?" He didn't want to say Dina's name because she would hear it and ask what they talked about. He hoped the soldiers did not understand English or would not be too interested in what they talked about.

Sawyer sighed. He knew he had made a mistake when he saved her in the forest. "I acted instinctively. I didn't think. I shouldn't have done it."

"We could have gotten rid of her back then and there," Jack whispered. "She's mortal now, and bullets can kill her."

"I know. I'm sorry. I made a mistake," Sawyer hissed back.

"I hope you aren't infatuated with her. You know that her body is just a shell, although pretty. The demon is inside it," Jack commented.

"I know," Sawyer muttered.

Lillian had tried to listen to what the guys were talking about, but she couldn't hear much of anything because of the noise of the truck's engine and the tires' sound on the gravel road. She hoped they had cooked up a plan for how to get rid of Dina now that she was mortal, but the problem was: so were they. Any shooting and they would all die, not just Dina.

The truck continued its travel uphill, and the passengers swung from side to side when the truck took steep turns. After fifteen minutes of driving, they reached the edge of the forest. The truck drove around the parking lot and parked in front of the barracks where the SS soldiers guarding Hitler were stationed.

53

The Prisoners

Dina was anxious, and she kept picking the hem of her skirt with her fingers. She didn't pay attention to Jack and Sawyer or worry about their whispering. Her thoughts were solely on Anubis. What if Anubis broke his promise again and took her before her time on Earth was done? There was no way to demand that Anubis keep his promise. He was the God of the underworld.

When the truck stopped in front of the barracks, Lillian woke up from her thoughts. She lifted her head and saw the soldiers get up and, one after another, jump down from the truck bed. The last one ordered, "Prisoners, come down one at a time."

Dina put on her high-heeled shoes, got up, and brushed her skirt with her hand. Next, she walked to the edge of the truck bed and waited for a soldier to help her down. None of them moved. They just stared at her. She commanded, "Help me down!"

When the soldiers stared at her, not even understanding what she said, she held out her hand, and a cobra appeared in the air with his mouth wide open and his teeth dripping with venom, she waved her hand, and the cobra attacked the closest soldier and bit him on his face. The soldier screamed and tried to pull away the snake, but he fell to the ground and writhed in pain. The cobra curled on his chest and raised his head, ready for the next victim.

The other soldiers stared at the snake and the soldier in pain and backed away. The officer who had captured them back in the woods ran to see what the screams were all about. When he saw the cobra curled on the body of a dead soldier, he took out his Walther P-38 and shot the snake. It vanished as if it had never existed, but the soldier stayed dead. His eyes stared up, horrified, and his face had red, swollen marks of a snake bite. The officer turned and saw Dina standing by the truck's bed, her fingers raised. The officer stared at Dina, surprised, and Dina glared back with her black emotionless eyes. Dina was ready to strike again when she felt a light touch on her shoulder.

"No, don't," Lillian said behind Dina, explaining, "They didn't understand what you said. Let Sawyer help you down." Lillian glanced back, and Sawyer and Jack stood up and came to stand next to the women. Jack and Sawyer jumped down and then held out their hands to help Dina and Lillian down from the truck bed.

"More tricks," the officer commented, viewing them suspiciously. "I saw the snake, and when I shot it, it disappeared. One of the soldiers is dead because of you." He turned his angry eyes to Dina. "I think we need to go inside and find out what's going on." He turned and marched in front of them to the barracks. The soldiers followed them a few feet behind.

They were taken through roughly built wooden quarters. The first one seemed to be for guards, and the next room was for receiving messages, as there was a radio operator and many telephones installed. The following room was for officers. The hallway ended in a hallway with five cells with bars on doors. Jack and Sawyer were pushed inside one cell and the women to the next one. The guard closed and locked the doors.

The officer marched in front of the cells and viewed them. Then he said, "Let's take that man." He pointed at Sawyer.

Two soldiers came behind the officer, opened the cell door, and took Sawyer with them.

Dina stared at the operation with no emotion. She had no idea what was going on.

Lillian screamed, "No, please, don't hurt him. He does not know anything. We hired him to fly us from Cairo. That's all he knows."

When he heard that, the officer lifted his hand and turned his cold eyes to Lillian. "It seems that you know more." He gestured with his fingers, and the soldiers returned Sawyer to his cell with Jack, and then they opened the door where Lillian and Dina were. They grabbed Lillian by her arms and pulled her out of the cell.

"Please, no," she cried, terrified, and tried to pull her arms away from the iron grip of the soldiers with no luck. She had heard what the Nazis did in interrogation.

Jack grabbed the bars on his cell door and interrupted. "You know you could just call Reichsführer Himmler. He knows who we are and why we are here."

"Ach, Reichsführer's office warned us of spies," the officer replied, giving Jack a lopsided smile.

"Did he also tell you what Dina can do?" When the officer hesitated, Jack pressed on, "He did tell you, didn't he?"

He raised his voice and said loudly, aiming his words at the soldiers listening, "Dina can kill you all. She does not need any guns to do that. You saw it back in the woods and outside in the parking lot. Do you want to mess with us, or do you want to find out what she wants?" He turned his eyes to the officer and said, "Call Himmler and ask what he wants us to do."

The officer did not like to take orders from a prisoner. He stared at Jack for a moment, considering if he should do like he said or not. Then he gestured to the guards. "Take the woman back to the cell."

Lillian sobbed as the soldiers pushed her back inside the cell with Dina.

Dina had not moved or done anything to help Lillian. She had just observed the situation like an outsider. Lillian turned to her and said, upset, "Why didn't you help me? I'm your translator."

Dina raised her eyebrows. "I'm not here to help slaves. I'm here to find the heart stone. All slaves can be replaced."

Lillian shook her head. "Not many understand your ancient language. You were lucky to find me."

Dina considered that for a moment and nodded. "I will keep you alive for now."

She looked around and saw a cot on the side of the cell and walked there and sat down. "Are they going to bring me the heart stone here?"

Lillian looked surprised. Dina did not seem to realize they were imprisoned. No one would treat them like guests and bring them anything voluntarily. "No, I don't think they will. I don't believe they know what you are looking for," Lillian replied. "You are the only one who knows what your scarab looks like." She hoped that the explanation was good enough to keep Dina calm.

Dina nodded. "They should let us go find it. I can identify the scarab."

Jack interrupted from his cell. "I think the officer went to call Himmler now. We'll see what they want to do with us."

The officer returned after ten minutes. He walked with long strides and stopped in front of the cells. He placed his arms behind his back and stood there staring at the prisoners. "I called Reichsführer's office. I have an offer for you. If the supernatural being comes to our side in this war, we will give her the artifact she is looking for." His eyes moved to Dina and then to Lillian. "One of you is the demon they mentioned. I guess it is you." His gaze stopped on Dina.

Jack quickly replied, "Yes, she is the demon. If you give her the scarab, she will rule the world. I don't think she will care for humanity or any petty wars between the different countries. You've seen what she can do."

The officer said, "Translate her what I said."

Lillian sighed and translated to Dina, who only laughed at it. "I don't need anyone. When I have the scarab on my hand, I will be a god on earth."

Jack rolled his eyes. They knew she would say that. Why did they keep asking? Himmler had heard the answer already in Berlin.

When Lillian translated the reply to the officer, he didn't look pleased. "I've been told to take you all in front of the firing squad if the answer is no."

Lillian turned to Dina and said, "They will shoot us all. Do something. You will die too if they do that. You are no longer an immortal."

Dina frowned. She remembered that. Anubis had transformed her into a mortal. She didn't even have her mummies left, but she had other tricks. She lifted both her hands and mumbled. The black beetles appeared from under her sleeves and her skirt and skittered to the officer and the guards ran up their legs and dug under their skins. Soon, the cries of pain and terror echoed as the beetles ate the officer and the two guards alive.

When the beetles finished, they returned to Dina and disappeared.

The noises had alerted the other soldiers, who came to check on what was happening.

When Dina saw them, she gestured with her hands, and the soldiers grabbed their throats as if invisible hands were strangling them. They fell to the floor, their faces dark purple.

No one else came after these soldiers. It was eerily quiet. They heard the squeaks and rings of the radio and phones, but no one answered. That meant only one thing: the operator was among the dead too. The building was empty.

"We still have a problem," Jack said, shaking the door of his cell. "We are locked inside here. How do we get out?" He was not in a hurry to escape the prison. The more time they used, the better for them, but he also realized that someone would soon start missing the dead officer and soldiers, especially since no one was answering the phones and the radio. This was the guard barracks of the Fuhrer's residence, and they would not let him be exposed to any danger, not when they knew who the latest prisoners here were.

54

Osiris

Dina saw Jack checking the door. She knew how to get out but was unsure if she should let the others go. They had not been helpful since Cairo. Now, it seemed they were more in her way than helping her. The Germans helped her to get here faster, but now it was time to act and not waste time.

Jack shook the bars on the doors, but it was sturdy, and he could not get any bars to move. Sawyer surveyed their cell to see if there was any other way to break the door. "Nothing. We are stuck until someone comes here." He sat on the cot facing Jack. "At least they won't suspect us killing everyone. We are behind bars and locked in the cells," Sawyer added.

"Himmler knows what Dina can do. They have the proof from the airport," Jack commented. "I don't want to be here when the Germans find out what happened." He frowned and viewed the door again. "If we could loosen the bars from either end, we could maybe make a big enough hole for us to get through," Jack said.

While the men were considering their options to escape, Dina shook her hands, and a swarm of beetles emerged. She mumbled something and gestured to the guard on the ground with the door's key in his hand. The beetles rushed to the guard and picked up the key to carry it on their elytra. They returned to Dina carrying the key, and she picked it up, opened the door, and slid outside, leaving Lillian inside.

Jack and Sawyer stepped to the door and shook it. "Hey, what about us? Are you leaving us behind?"

Dina gave them a disgruntled look and said, "You were helpful back in Cairo, but after that, you have not carried your weight." She gave Sawyer a longing gaze and added, "I hope we will meet again. I would have enjoyed spending nights with you, Sawyer." She sent him an air kiss and walked out.

"Lillian, are you okay?" Jack asked. Lillian came to her cell door and said, "Yes, I'm fine. This was a surprise. I didn't think she would leave us here."

"Neither did we." Sawyer brushed his hair back from his forehead. "What do we do now?"

"Get out. We can't let Dina get that scarab." Jack went back to the door and tried to loosen the bars from the bottom and then from the top. "Help me. Maybe we can get one of the bars loose."

Sawyer shook his head. "No, I don't think so. These Germans have made a good-quality prison here. We can't break the door." He stared at the bodies lying on the floor. "Other soldiers and the officers might have another set of keys. Can we drag one of the bodies closer?"

"We can try to make a loop with our belts and pull the closest one toward us," Jack said, took out his belt, made a loop of it, and then attached it to Sawyer's belt.

After several unsuccessful throws, the loop went around the dead man's hand, and Jack pulled it carefully closer. When it was near enough, both men reached through the bars and pulled the rest of the way. Then they searched through his pockets and found another set of keys. They fumbled with the set of keys and tried each on the lock.

"Dina had it easier. She took the only key that we saw working on the locks. We don't know if any of these keys work," Jack grumbled.

Sawyer tried the next one, and this time, the lock clicked, and he pushed the door open. Then he used the same key to Lillian's door and let her out.

They snuck through the hallway and past the empty rooms. "Where do you think Dina is?" Lillian asked with a hushed voice.

Sawyer glared ahead and said, "She might be recruiting more help or on her way up in the elevator."

Then the air dimmed like a large shadow blanketed the hallway.

Lillian backed against the wall, and the men stood still.

"You will stop Dina. She cannot have the scarab in her hands," a powerful voice echoed in the hallway. "The world will not be the same if she lives."

"We don't know how to stop her," Lillian replied, although she didn't know whom she was answering. Then she saw a bull-headed shadow. She realized a new god had entered their world: Osiris, whose symbol was often a bull.

"I, Osiris, will not allow the future to be changed by her and Anubis. You will have the power to stop Dina when the time comes," Osiris said cryptically. "You have time. She is not in the elevator yet."

The hallway brightened again, and the shadow faded away.

Lillian looked at her company and said, "Osiris is the god of the dead and fertility. It seems that the underworld is not pleased with Anubis and Dina."

"I don't see how that will help us," Sawyer said. "Osiris didn't say where Dina is or how we can defeat her."

Jack was quiet for a moment, then said, "I think I know. She will have to use the elevator to go up. We need to destroy the elevator or stall it so that she will not reach the top before her time on Earth ends. That's how we do it."

He looked at the others, who nodded.

55

The Elevator

When Dina left the prison cells, she walked through the barracks making sure no one of the soldiers was alive. Outside, she sent her beetles to destroy the two last guards she saw guarding the safety of the elevator passage. She knew that led upwards because they had seen the visitors going up when surveying the area from the woods.

She walked casually to the passage that led inside the mountain where the elevator was. The electric lights gave a dim light in the tunnel. It didn't take her long to walk to the end of it.

There she saw a door with buttons on the side. She tried to open it. It didn't open because the elevator was up. She frowned. How could she get up? She had heard the others say this was the way to go up. They were talking about a lift going upwards. She looked at the buttons next to the door and pressed one. A buzzing sound came, and she heard a clonking sound. Something moved. She stood there waiting for the sound to come closer.

When it stopped, Dina tried the door again. This time it opened. She looked inside. The walls were made of shiny brass and the seats were green velvet. It looked comfortable, so she went to sit there. Nothing happened. She looked around and saw a button on the wall by the door. She pressed the bottom one, and nothing happened. Then she tried the top one, and the elevator jerked and started ascending at a slow speed.

She smiled and sat down. *Soon, I will possess the scarab, and the world will be mine until the end of time,* she thought victoriously.

While Dina had walked inside the passage leading to the elevator and figured out how to use the elevator, the other prisoners had escaped and met Osiris. Now, the three of them ran to the elevator passage and reached the door, but Dina was already going up.

"She's in the elevator," Jack said, craning his neck.

"She is not up yet. We can stop it." Jack said and pressed the other button next to the elevator door. It didn't work. He had hoped that by pressing the button again, the elevator would stop and descend.

"Where does the electricity come from?" Sawyer asked, looking around. "If we stop the power, she can't reach the top level." His eyes followed the wires on the wall, leading to a box on the wall. He ran there and opened the box. Inside, he found an on/off switch. He pulled it to the off position, and the humming of the elevator stopped with a screech. The elevator was stopped in the middle of the shaft going upwards.

Silent darkness fell over the shaft. Sawyer, Jack, and Lillian waited in the tunnel staring upward, and it didn't take long before they heard Dina scream. She cursed the metal box she was in. They heard her kicking the door and banging it with her fists. She was mortal now, but she was not to be underestimated. They heard the clicking sound of the beetles as they pushed through the elevator and ran around the elevator walls. The beetles scurried around, but they could not get the elevator to start. It needed the power.

"That was the beetles," Jack said. "What else can she try? The snakes won't help, and neither will the strangling hands. She can't start the electricity from inside the elevator."

"Did we find a way to beat her?" Lillian asked, almost smiling.

"It seems so," Sawyer replied and placed his arm around her shoulders.

"When do you think her time is up?" Jack asked, still glaring at the darkness of the elevator shaft.

"I think it will be a few more hours before her time ends. We need to be here to make sure no one turns on the electricity before that," Lillian replied. "We met her around noonish in the archeological excavation site, and she had been awakened hours before. I would guess the archeologists started early that morning, perhaps seven or eight o'clock, and that's when she was awakened."

"Can we wait here a few more hours? Do you think the Germans will come?" Sawyer asked, glancing back in the direction where they had entered the shaft.

"I don't know. I would guess they will send more soldiers when no one answers the phone calls or the radio. It might take a couple of hours before they get the next troop here," Jack said.

"We have to cut off the electricity so that the elevator does not start up until tomorrow," Sawyer said, checking the electricity box where the electricity was turned on and off. "Can we break this?"

Jack walked over to him. It was hard to see anything in the dark. "If we can find a dynamite, we could blow that up," Jack replied. "Or perhaps we can just shoot it?"

"Could we pull off all the wires and cut them, so no one can start the elevator?" Lillian asked behind them.

"We need a flashlight. I can go and get one from the barracks. I think all the soldiers had one," Jack said, then ran outside and in the direction of the barracks. He returned soon with three flashlights and three utility knives.

He handed two of them to Lillian and Sawyer, and then Jack and Sawyer unscrewed the box and took the electricity box off the wall, cutting the wires while Lillian showed the light to the box. When the inside of the electricity box was a mess of cut wires, they stopped.

"Do you think that's enough for several hours?" Jack asked.

"Yes, I think so. The Germans will have to replace all the wires. I don't think they have a storage of extra wires here. It will take them hours to fix this. We can go now." Sawyer folded his knife and put it in his pocket.

When the three of them left, the moon was shining. It was past midnight.

As Lillian thought, there were seven hours left of Dina's time on earth.

Even if the Germans arrived in a couple of hours, it would take time to repair the electricity box.

"Are you sure that's enough?" Lillian asked when they were outside.

Jack looked at her and said, "We can also drive some cars in front of the passageway and block it that way. And if we break their engines, it will be even harder for Germans to get inside and start fixing the electricity."

"Let's do that," Lillian said. "I want to be sure Dina won't have time to get the scarab."

They drove two jeeps inside the tunnel, pulled out wires and sparkplugs, and walked outside.

Lillian waited in the third jeep. "Let's go before the Nazis arrive," she said.

Jack jumped into the driver's seat with Sawyer next to him. Lillian sat on the back. As they drove through the gate, everything was eerily quiet. No one was guarding the area where Fuhrer had his residence and where he met important visitors.

56

THE GERMANS

Jack didn't have time to drive very far when bright headlights climbed up the mountainside and blinded Jack. He stopped his vehicle. "We are caught!" he muttered.

There was no way to go around. If the vehicle in front wanted to shoot them, they could. He cursed. He should have taken a machine gun or a pistol. There were plenty of them available on the bodies.

"Don't shoot!" Jack shouted in German to the oncoming vehicle.

"We don't plan to. We came to look for you," a familiar voice replied. It was Carl Bosch.

Jack lowered his hands. *What is the industrialist doing here?* he wondered. He got out of his car and walked to meet Carl, and when he got to the incoming vehicle, he saw that Carl was accompanied by the two other men: Alfried Krupp and Friedrich Flick.

He stopped next to Carl, pushed his hands into his pockets, and asked, "What are you guys doing here? I thought you would go back home when Dina left you by the roadside."

Carl snorted. "We were taken to Himmler's office and questioned there. After that, we thought about going home, but the threat of Dina conquering this world was too great, so we decided to drive here to see if we could help."

Jack gestured towards the camp area behind his jeep and said, "All the soldiers are dead. No one back there is alive. That was all Dina's doing."

"Where is she?" Alfried asked from the back seat.

"We trapped her inside the elevator in the shaft. We broke the electricity box and cut all the wires, so it will take some time for anyone to fix it. Also, we parked two cars in the passageway, took out their sparkplugs, and cut some wires, so they wouldn't be moved out easily. I just hope that's enough," Jack replied, glancing back to the tunnel where Dina was trapped.

"Do you think she can get out?" Carl asked, his hands gripping tighter on the steering wheel. He remembered well how Dina had killed soldiers before at the airport, and now she had killed the personnel of this camp too.

"I can't be sure. I hope not," Jack replied. ". She is stuck in the elevator halfway up. There's no other way to get up there as far as I know. We heard hundreds of beetles scurrying around. They are small enough to escape the elevator cabin. She'll keep looking for a way out and if her beetles can help, then we can't do anything," Jack replied.

Friedrich interrupted. "I have a coal mine close by. We drove by that site earlier before coming here. We have dynamite with us. We can blow up the entrance to the shaft, and if the explosion is right under her, then it might shake the elevator so that it will be permanently damaged or stuck, or it might crash down."

Jack felt a jolt of excitement inside him. "That's a brilliant idea." He slammed his palm on the hood and added, "Anubis made Dina mortal. She can't control the mummies, but she can command her beetles and snakes. Because she is mortal, she can die in an explosion like any human."

Carl glanced at Alfried and Friedrich who both nodded. "Let's go and blow up that mountain tunnel."

Jack ran to his jeep and backed it into the parking area and Carl followed with his vehicle. Jack explained to Sawyer and Lillian what the new plan was.

Friedrich pulled out his stack of dynamite and put a long detonating cord on it, long enough to reach from the entrance of the tunnel to the elevator shaft. They placed a couple of sticks of dynamite right under the elevator shaft. Friedrich glanced up using his flashlight and saw the bottom of the elevator higher up. He shivered. "Dina's there isn't she?" he asked Jack who nodded and replied, "Yes, let's do this. No time to waste."

Friedrich backed slowly pulling behind him the detonation cord and Jack showed him the light. When they reached outside, he took out the matchbox and asked, "Is everyone ready?"

Jack motioned to the others, and yelled, "Get ready to go."

Friedrich lit the detonation cord and ran after Jack who went to the driver's seat of his jeep, and Friedrich ran to the backseat of Carl's vehicle.

They drove outside the gate and downwards when the explosion echoed. Jack glimpsed back and saw the tunnel's entrance covered with smoke and dust.

They felt a cold blast of wind and like hands touching them and heard a frustrated and angry wail in the air. "That's Dina," Lillian said and shivered. "She's dead."

Lillian was right. The power of the blast in a tight space caused the elevator to drop, and Dina died in the explosion.

Anubis appeared to her in her last moment on Earth. "Dina, you'll return with me to the underworld. You lost your chance to rule this world."

Dina hissed, "Only because you took away some of my powers and I was no longer in control of the undead."

Anubis's jackal head grew bigger, and he growled, "Are you blaming me, the god of the underworld?"

Dina didn't answer. She took her last breath and died. Her soul parted her human body traveled in the air and followed Anubis back to his kingdom.

After the explosion, both cars drove down the hill and when they reached the edge of the village, Carl stopped and waited for Jack to drive next to him.

Friedrich said, "Jack, I have the mine close by. If you follow us there, I have a small airplane you can use. Sawyer can fly it."

"Thank you. We never had time to think how to get out of the country after Dina's death," Jack replied and drove after Carl.

They reached the mining compound in fifteen minutes. Carl drove near the building and behind it was a Junker Ju-52 airplane. "That's a beauty," Sawyer said assessing the airplane. It was big enough for the three of them.

"I hope you know how to fly that and where to go," Friedrich said and extended his hand. Sawyer shook it. "Thank you. I know how to fly any aircraft. I think we'll head toward Switzerland. I hope we won't meet any German planes on the way there."

"It's a German-manufactured plane, so I don't think that will be a problem. Besides, the military knows I have planes here to test drive purposes, so they won't bother you," Friedrich replied.

Jack, Sawyer, and Lillian said goodbyes to the German businessmen and headed to the airplane. In no time, Sawyer got the plane on the runway and then up in the air.

"Time to go home," he said.

"Good idea," Lillian replied smiling.

Jack looked out through the window. He saw a row of jeeps approaching further away and heading to the mountain where they had left. "We got out just in time. The Nazis are coming to check out their camp."

"They won't find anyone alive there to tell what happened. Dina is dead too," Lillian replied.

"I know, we are safe and so is the world." Jack leaned back and closed his eyes.

About the Author

Meet Arla Jones, a multi-genre author hailing from the picturesque landscapes of Finland, now making waves in the literary world from the tranquil shores of Michigan. With a penchant for exploring diverse genres, the author captivates readers with tales that traverse the realms of mystery, romance, thriller, sci-fi, and fantasy, weaving intricate narratives that transport audiences to worlds both familiar and fantastical. When not penning captivating stories, the author enjoys gardening and painting.

Also By The Author

Some of these are published as serial fiction and some are available in different formats.

The Starbound Orphans Series: (YA/Sci-Fi)

Starbound Orphans

Starbound Journey

Starbound Hearts

The Galactic Emperor (coming soon)

The Ackley Family Saga:

Lord Ackley's Choice

A Rose So Red

Court of Kisses

A Romance Short story:

Snowbound Strangers

Jaxon Axis -series (Dystopian, Sci-Fi):

Jaxon Axis and the First Crime

Jaxon Axis and the Ice Age

The Lost Tomb -series:

The Lost Tomb

Venemous Dunes

The Lost Oasis of Love

The Mummy Returns

The Otis Thorne Thriller series:

Fathers and Sons

Black Dust

The Facility

Death Walks in Washington D.C.

The Ashburn -series

On Death's Door

Finders Keepers

The Kingdom Series (fantasy, romantasy, YA)

Wings of Sea

Wings of War

Wings of Shadows

Westerns

The Lady and The Stubborn Rancher

The Lady and The Robber Baron

Bury My Dreams

The Cupid and the Elf -series:

Love Trap

Naughty Elf

Ghost Stories

The Cursed Banshee

Don't Go There

Sci-Fi

The Host

Titanic Paranormal Novel

Chasing Death

Children's books:

The Attack of the Iguana

Evil Elves

The Underground Cat Academy

Bobbie Robins Contemporary thrillers:

Samantha Raven Trilogy:

I'll Be Your Shadow

I'll Never Let You Go

I'll Be Back

Ayla Jones (Dark Romance)

Donder

Bloodlines of Revolution

No Way But Down

Dragon Unleashed

Bloodlines of Revolution

Anthologies:

The Tales of Howloween

Find a full list of serial fiction, novels, and my shop: arlajones.com

And also https://beacons.ai/arlajonesbooks

Tiktok: @jonesesbooks and @authorarlajones

Facebook: www.facebook.com/authorarlajones

Instagram: https://www.instagram.com/arlajonesbooks